Secrets of the Moon

Tema Encarnación

ISBN-13: 9781986771481

Library of Congress Control Number: 2018904136

This is a work of fiction. All of the characters, names, incidents, organizations, and dialogue in this novel are either products of the author's imagination or are used fictitiously.

Dedication

To my mother. Your beautifully unapologetic example has guided me in my own imperfect journey. Your sacrifices have not gone unnoticed. Your unending encouragement gives me strength.

And to the generations of immigrants who have woven, and are weaving, their lives, experiences, and stories into the fabric of the United States. Your stories of strength, courage, and perseverance inspire me every day. Thank you for allowing me to tell one of them.

Give me your tired, your poor,
Your huddled masses yearning to breathe free,
The wretched refuse of your teeming shore.
Send these, the homeless, tempest-tossed to me,
I lift my lamp beside the golden door!

- Emma Lazarus

"Sé muy bien lo que tengo planeado para ustedes," dice el Señor, "son planes para su bienestar, no para su mal. Son planes de darles un futuro y una esperanza."

- Jeremías 29:11

"For I know the plans I have for you," declares the Lord, "plans to prosper you and not to harm you, plans to give you hope and a future."

- Jeremiah 29:11

Prologue

Luz

My eyes opened abruptly as the rooster squawked one of his early-morning frenzied songs. It was still dark, but I could see—between the rusted tin roof and the old cinder block walls—that the light was changing as the day approached. The sun's rays slowly crept in, and I started to distinguish the delicate pink paint chipping off of my bedroom wall. The images on the faded lacquered pictures that adorned my room became visible, and faces of extended family members graduating from high school and getting married stared back at me through their encapsulated frames. The dusty stuffed animals, *peluches,* that I had collected over the years watched over me from the shelves above. I smiled as I remembered how I had acquired each one.

This was one of the many times I woke up since going to bed the night before. Anticipating the day ahead of me, my mind raced, and every time I fell asleep, I startled awake just minutes later. My excitement overwhelmed me that morning. I knew this day's sunrise would be the start of my new life, but my twelve-year-old mind couldn't wrap itself around what the day would bring.

My *abuelita*, who must have heard me stirring across the flimsy cardboard-like wall that separated our bedrooms, called out for me to stay calm and to go back to sleep. She reminded me, in a raspy, sleepy whisper that I wouldn't be of use to anyone if I were too tired for the trip.

"Yes," I simply replied.

I had been waiting for this day since I was six years old—over half of my life. How could my *abuelita* expect me to sleep calmly?

Six years ago, almost to the day, my mother kissed me gently on the forehead and told me that she would be going to the city for a few days and that she would return soon. Even after all those years, the memory of her leaving me was as vivid as if it had just happened. I had just started school in my *campo,* my village, but my mother's leaving cast a dark shadow of what should have been a happy time. Her last moments with me are still seared in my memory.

As she said goodbye, I remember pouting at her because I always loved going on the bus to the city. I loved going on any adventure with my *mami*, and the thought that she would leave me behind insulted my six-year-old sensibilities. "Bye, *mami*," I said reluctantly, maybe even bitterly, as I stubbornly peeled myself away from her as she tried to give me one last hug.

Many times after she had left, I thought back to that exchange and reimagined it. In each remembrance, instead of showing her my anger and petulance, I would hug and hold her tightly.

What if I had done that instead? Would she have stayed with me that day? Over the years, I wondered if maybe I made it easier for her to leave me. If I had known that I wouldn't see her for six years, I'm certain I would have given her a more loving goodbye. But she didn't give me that chance.

Shortly after she left, I began anxiously asking my grandmother when *mamá* would return. "Soon," *abuelita* kept telling me, trying to sound confident, but her hesitancy made me think differently. I know *abuelita* wanted to make me feel at ease after *mami* left, but her simple, curt responses made me feel otherwise, each time she uttered them. I felt her nervousness.

Now I know that what she was hiding, or trying to hide, was the fear a mother feels when her child is in danger. Like a mother lion watching her cub take his first timid steps out of the den, my grandmother knew that her daughter was on a necessary yet dangerous journey. Her longing to protect her young was overwhelming her. At the time, all I knew was that something was not right.

As my *abuelita* lay in her bed, listening to my early-morning jitters, she must have been feeling the same fear and dread that she had felt for my mother. It must have been unbearable for her, first losing her daughter, and then her granddaughter, to what was supposed to be a dream. Having invested a lifetime raising them, and then losing them to an unknown future.

I didn't understand, know, or even really care what my *abuelita* must have been experiencing. All I knew, that breezy, balmy morning, was that I was leaving my *campo* in El Salvador to make a new life in *los Estados Unidos*. Very soon, I would meet my mother again and would finally give her the hug that I had withheld so many years ago. I would apologize for not hugging her like that, the day she left.

I couldn't even imagine how *mami* might be, now. I wondered if I would recognize her. Did she look the same as I remembered her? Would she recognize me, her twelve-year-old daughter?

Lying there, looking at the picture of her hanging on my bedroom wall and waiting for the day to begin, I longed to see her. My heart physically ached, thinking about reuniting.

As the rooster crowed again, it became evident that I would not get back to sleep that morning. I slipped quietly out of my bed. My *abuelita* had also emerged from her room and was rustling around in the kitchen.

As I washed my face, the sweet smell of plantains, eggs frying, and the rich aroma of coffee delicately spiced with cinnamon permeated our small *campo*-style house. *Abuelita* invited me to the table for my favorite breakfast, one she had prepared just for me. Although I loved this farewell meal, I could barely eat, as waves of nausea overtook me. A few minutes after sitting down, I asked *abuelita* to excuse me from the table. I got up, gagging slightly and coughing as I felt my throat tighten. I walked quickly to a far corner of the backyard, behind a large banana tree, and threw up the few bites of breakfast that my *abuelita* had so lovingly prepared. Then I prayed that she had not seen this happen.

A bit later, I gathered my backpack, which I had packed and repacked several times over the last few days, and waited nervously on our front porch. I sat on the railing, drawing circles with the toe of my shoe in the dusty dirt road. I listened to *abuelita* inside, humming to herself. She often did this as she cleaned up the kitchen, but on this day I heard her hesitancy.

Although she tried to complete her typical routine as if this were a day like any other, the dishes clanked with a bit more force than normal. She would never admit it, but I knew she was at least as nervous as I was. Nevertheless, she put on her strong face and was stoic for what must have been one of the hardest days of her life. She was a rock.

Suddenly, she stopped humming. She had heard it, and so had I. It was the grating, grinding sound of the laden tires of a pickup truck charging down our tiny dirt road. We heard it often, about ten or fifteen times a day. But today, it was different. We knew this truck was headed toward our house. The old red pickup, coming full speed toward us, would carry me away from the only life I had ever known. We heard the truck in the distance, but it was still about thirty seconds from rounding the bend and arriving at our house.

Slowly, my *abuelita* walked toward the front porch, drying her hands on a dirty dish towel. She stood behind me where I was sitting and put her damp hand on my shoulder. I looked up and back and could see her other hand brush across her cheek as she sniffled ever so slightly. The rumbling sound of the truck grew louder. We could now see the cloud of dust that enveloped it as it recklessly sped down the dirt path. It stopped abruptly and hurriedly in front of my house, the only house that I'd ever lived in.

About seven or eight people stared back at us as they sat in the bed of the pickup. I could feel my grandmother's hand squeeze my shoulder and gently hold onto me as I nervously yet purposefully stood up. The truck driver threw open the door, got out, and started strutting around. He reminded me of the rooster, crowing about, proud without reason.

I turned to my *abuelita* and looked at her watery, bloodshot eyes. She suddenly looked very old and feeble. Her short grey hair, matted from resting on her pillow, was flattened in the back and stood up, almost making a halo around her head. I hugged her tightly, wrapping my arms around her frail frame, and told her how much I loved her. I couldn't live with the guilt of another halfhearted farewell and kissed her gently on her wrinkled cheek.

As I turned to get in the back of the truck with the other passengers, my *abuelita* talked to the rooster-man, with his cocky stance and supersized belly hanging over his belt. She put her hand on his back, as if they were old friends, and they both turned away from the truck. They were talking, but I couldn't make out what they were saying. Then they both turned back around, and the rooster-man slipped something into his pocket as he got back in the truck.

We quickly pulled away from my house as my grandmother stood alone, waving goodbye. Her halo of hair made her look like the angel I was finally realizing that she was.

As we pulled away and the dust from the road enveloped us, panic overcame me. I felt numb, my heart pounded, and the nausea returned. I looked at my fellow passengers, each with a story and reasons for leaving everything behind. There was a boy of about fifteen, old enough to leave home and look for work to do his part to support his family. I had seen him at school, but couldn't remember his name. He was a few grades ahead of me. He must have recognized me, too, because he studied my face. Next to him sat a young mother, holding her infant son, probably going to meet the child's father after a long and desperate separation. I looked across the truck at an older couple holding hands. They were dressed in their Sunday best and still obviously in love after a lifetime together. I looked at three other kids who were about my age, and I knew they were feeling as I was.

I looked at each of the passengers again, this time scrutinizing their faces. Then I could see it—the look in their eyes, just as I imagined the look in my eyes—fear, excitement, dread, and hope.

One

Luz

About a month after *mami* left, she called and left a message with a neighbor. There was only one phone in the *campo*, and days without electricity meant communication was painfully inconsistent. Messages were left when and where they could be. When my grandmother received the message, her chest rose and fell slowly as she exhaled a much-needed sigh of relief. Her eyes softened as she closed them, and she lifted her face to the sky as if saying a quick but grateful "thank-you" to God. An emotional weight had lifted, now that she received word that her daughter was safe.

Two days later, my grandmother took me to the *pueblo,* the closest town to our *campo,* and we used the phone in the pharmacy to call the number *mami* had left with our neighbor. *Abuelita* couldn't read, and I had yet to learn, so we asked the girl at the pharmacy counter to dial what seemed like an endless list of digits. In her light blue button-down shirt, she smelled of overly sweet flowery perfume. Smiling gently at us, a gap between her two front teeth revealed itself.

"Who are we calling today?" she asked my *abuelita* lightly, sensing my grandmother's anxiety about the impending call, hoping to soothe it with small talk.

"Aaahh," my grandmother hesitated slightly, "I'm calling my daughter, she's gone to *el Norte*, she's in *los Estados Unidos.*"

I could hardly believe what I had just heard. I'd been resting my chin on the glass counter, looking longingly at the dolls inside the display case, imagining each of their names and inventing elaborate stories of their lives. My chin made a squeaking, thudding noise as I yanked it across the glass to inspect my grandmother's face. I was shocked at this declaration. What had she just said? *¿El Norte? ¿Estados Unidos?*

Even at six-years-old I knew that going to *el Norte* wasn't an everyday occurrence. I'd heard the stories of people fleeing the dangers of El Salvador, going north to work, earning money to send to their families back home, bringing their family, one person at a time, to join them in the United States. They dreamed of coming back one day as old men and women. Some of my friends' moms and dads had gone to *los Estados Unidos.* They sent back money and little presents, but I couldn't remember ever having seen them again.

11

My friends talked about their parents being in *el Norte* with a sense of pride, but I always knew they were also very sad to be so far from them. How could they not be?

My *abuelita* must have been confused that day, because my mother told me that she had gone to the city. That's where my *mamá* was. I stood aghast, staring at my grandmother with my mouth agape and my chin now itching and red from its encounter with the glass. She looked sideways, down her nose at me, trying her best not to make eye contact.

"Yes," said the attendant with her gap-toothed grin. "You must be very proud. Let's see that number."

As the attendant passed the receiver to my grandmother, I got another whiff of her sweet perfume; this time, I gagged at the scent. I heard the muffled ring of the telephone as *abuelita* pressed it against her ear with both hands, afraid to let it slip away as her daughter had but one month earlier.

"*Hallo, hallo…*" A pause.

My grandmother's chest rose and fell heavily.

"*Ay, mi'ja,*" she said with a whisper of relief as a tear rolled down her cheek and a smile filled her face. I saw the anxiety fade away.

12

I heard my mother's muffled voice on the other end of the line. She spoke quickly and loudly to my *abuelita*, whose tears flowed more freely.

Abuelita's face started turning red, and her voice cracked in an effort to keep from audibly weeping.

"*Sí, sí*," she said occasionally, probably the only thing that she could utter without exploding into tears.

After a few minutes, my grandmother hurriedly passed the phone to me and told me to talk with my mother.

"*Mami*," I said, suddenly angry and confused, and then confused about why I was angry. "Where are you?" I demanded.

"*Ay, mi amor*," she said, trying to comfort and distract me. "I'm in *los Estados Unidos*, and you're going to come and be with me as soon as I can earn enough money to bring you."

I was furious. I asked her why she didn't return from the city after her trip. Why she didn't take me with her. Why she waited so long to call. The longer we spoke, the angrier I became. Despite my anger, she responded quietly, calmly, never raising her voice. She didn't answer my questions. Instead she assured me that everything would be fine. I wanted to believe her. Everything inside of me wanted to believe her. But how could I trust her now?

We continued, back and forth, my angry scolding and her patient response. Several minutes passed. The line went dead.

I looked up at my grandmother, who was standing next to me. She had her chin in her hands, her elbows resting against the counter. She had listened as I scolded my mother. I still had the receiver against my ear, and I slowly lowered it to the counter. Then I banged it forcefully against the glass, hard enough to make a noise, but with enough restraint to keep from breaking it.

"I want my *mami!*" I want my *mami!*" I screamed, throwing the receiver across the counter. I grabbed my *abuelita* around her waist and hugged her, sobbing uncontrollably. She reached her arms around me and nestled her face in my hair.

I realized again that *abuelita* was upset, too, when her silent shaking gave her away. She was also crying. We held each other, grieving my mother's departure.

I don't know how long we stood there, both of us crying, but eventually she scooped me up into her arms and sat me on the counter. She wiped away my tears and told me that everything would be all right. I looked into her eyes

14

and saw her pain. I hugged her, and she carried me off the counter and walked with me in her arms to the bus stop. We waited silently for the bus to take us home.

On the ride back to the *campo*, it began to rain—one of those fierce tropical storms that comes mid-afternoon and dumps endless gallons of water onto everything in its path. Seated on the sticky plastic bus seats, I slouched against my *abuelita* and propped my foot up against the bus wall.

Staring out the window, the deep green mountains around us and the river flowing below, I kept repeating the conversation I'd had with my mother in my head. It was unnerving. As my whole world crumbled, her life was beginning again. I closed my eyes and kept hearing her calm voice echoing in my ears. The rain pounded the windows of the bus, and the constant, steady thud of the drops against the glass lulled me into a deep, deep sleep.

Two

Esperanza

The day I left my *campo* was the hardest day of my life. I left Luz with my mother—I knew that she would be in good hands. My mother loved her dearly, and I trusted her wholeheartedly to care for her just as I did.

I kissed Luz on the head and told her I would be back soon, that I was just going to the city. As I kissed her, I breathed in the sweet smell of her damp black hair and fixed in my mind the way the light hit it, how it glistened in the late afternoon sun, slightly blue in its darkness. She had just taken a bath after an afternoon swim in the river behind our house. Her skin was still cool and soft from the water. It was the way she felt when I put her to bed at night— clean and sweet.

Putting Luz to bed each night was one of the things I enjoyed most about motherhood, and at that moment, I knew I would miss that time with her the most. Every night, after she bathed, we'd snuggle in her bed, and I'd tell her silly stories about my day or my childhood until she fell asleep. As we snuggled up together, her skinny little matchstick legs and knobby knees would poke me in the belly. Sometimes she would shiver from the chill of the bath, and I would hug her tightly to warm her up. When she was feeling particularly loving, she would say that my hugs were the only thing that could keep her warm.

We started this routine when she was about a year old. I think I looked forward to its quiet calmness as much as she did. And even though I would never let her know, I'm sure I was sadder than she was each night when I left her bed to go to my own.

The night before I left for *el Norte*, we discovered that she had a loose tooth. I wiggled it and told her that I would cry when it finally fell out. She looked at me with a puzzled expression, so I explained that I was going to be sad to see my baby growing up into such a big kid. She giggled a nervous and then mischievous chuckle at the thought, and then grinned from ear to ear. I studied her face so as to never forget how she looked. Her expression in that moment so clearly captured her personality, agreeable yet playfully naughty. Pure satisfaction spread across her face, and I wanted to be sure that I would remember this clearly in my mind's eye.

She'll never know how often I retrieved her satisfied, smiling face from my memory. And she'll never imagine what calmness her sweet eyes gave me or what perseverance her mischievous smile inspired. There were days while I was traveling to *los Estados Unidos*, and many days after I arrived, when I would conjure up Luz's smile for comfort. Her little face, her light brown skin perfectly contrasting against her tattered white nightgown, her beautiful, tiny, wiggly teeth smiling back at me, encouraged me to press on. I had risked everything for that little girl, and if it was the last thing I ever did, I would be sure that she would be by my side again.

When I had become pregnant with Luz, I was certain that my life was following a predetermined plan that was divinely ordained by God the day I was born. From my years of going to mass with the Catholic missionary priests sent to my *campo*, I knew that God had a plan for my life and that this pregnancy was no accident.

Luz's father, Diego, had been a classmate of mine. We grew up together in the *campo* and shared many memories and experiences from school and around our community. We laughed at the same jokes, watched the same outdated, ridiculously dubbed American action movies, and sang along together to the same love songs. We were so comfortable with each other that it seemed natural when our friendship started to change. He was so gentle with me, and confident, that I couldn't help but be swayed by his persistent persuasion.

I was sixteen years old when I realized that Luz was on the way. I was afraid to tell my mother when I suspected that I was pregnant because I knew that she envisioned a different future for me. She always talked about me making a better life for myself. She wanted something different for me than our small *campo*.

When I finally told her that Diego and I would be parents, I saw the disappointment in her eyes as she realized that her hopes for me would have to change. She quickly resigned herself to the inevitable pattern that had repeated itself for generations in our family and in many other families in our *campo*. She couldn't be angry with me for something that was destined to happen. Eventually, as the pregnancy went on, she was very pleased that she would be a grandmother.

At first, Diego seemed happy and excited about being a father. He often patted my belly and came over to visit me and charm my mother. He promised her that he would take care of our baby and me. He promised me a future, and I believed him.

Things changed, though. The best-laid plans sometimes crumble into nothingness. Even more so when a sixteen-year-old girl is impregnated by her boyfriend in a country that people leave by the thousands every day in search of safety and stability. It didn't occur to me until much later that I was bringing a little person into a place that so many people were fleeing from. At the time, this paradox escaped me—in my naïveté, all I could imagine was marrying Diego and living happily ever after in our *campo*.

About midway through the pregnancy, Diego started changing. He realized that, if he was to be the father that he wanted to be, he couldn't do it in the *campo*. Working on someone else's farm will allow a man to provide day-to-day for his family, but it won't ever let a person get ahead. There is a system in our country that keeps the poor poor and the rich rich, and that's how it's been since the Spaniards arrived five hundred years ago. That wasn't going to change in our lifetimes, and so his immediate concern was making a life for our child.

In hopes of providing for our new family, Diego left for the city to find work. Assuring me that he would find something, he told me how talented he was and how anyone in the city would be glad to have him as an employee. He'd start off working for someone else, and then, when he was a little older and more experienced, he would start his own business.

I had been to the city maybe four times in my life. If Diego said it, it must have been true. I knew that he was smart and that he was a hard worker. He convinced me that things would be fine.

The day he left for the city, he kissed me gently on the forehead. I hugged him tightly and kissed him on his bristly cheek. He gently rubbed my belly, telling me to take care of his baby, and lowered his head to kiss his unborn child. As he lifted his head up to look me in the eyes, I squeezed his face and then wrapped my hands around the back of his head, bringing him close and pressing my cheek against his.

His leaving broke my heart into a million pieces. But we both knew that this was for the best, and the only way we could make a life for ourselves. Just like everything else, we knew that this, too, was inevitable.

God, how I loved Diego! There were never two people more meant for one another than he and I. He was my soul mate, and as I hugged him goodbye, I knew that God had sent us our child as a way of uniting us forever.

Three

Luz

Mami called pretty regularly. Through these calls, I would piece together the puzzle of her new life. At first, she told me about the grocery stores and how enormous they were. After she'd been there a few months, she spoke of the various places where she had been living and the friends she was making. Later, she talked about her different jobs, cleaning houses or working in restaurants, and the *Americanos* she came in contact with.

Sometimes the people she described seemed to be caricatures—so exaggeratedly different from what I knew, that any similarities would become so distorted, almost unrecognizable.

Her descriptions of other things were overwhelming, often unbelievable. She described how she lived, but it was all very hard to understand. Sometimes I felt like she had moved to another planet because everything sounded so foreign.

Mami talked about her *apartamento* inside a giant building. She described her neighbors and people living on all sides of her. I couldn't imagine hundreds of people living inside one building. I couldn't imagine the city streets she talked about, with so many cars on them that sometimes they couldn't move. All I knew were the wooden shacks and dirt roads of our *campo*.

She talked about grocery stores, with food from ceiling to floor. What could possibly be there for sale, when everything we needed could be sold from the roadside produce stand? Who were these people *mami* saw who ate dinner in restaurants every night? Babies in my *campo* ate only enough to feed the parasites in their bellies. How could the owners of the houses that *mami* cleaned throw away bags of perfectly good clothing? My classmates often missed years of school because the modest cost of a school uniform was out of reach.

Mamá tried to get me excited about going to *el Norte* to be with her and enjoy all the comforts of this "land of opportunity." Sometimes I would get very excited and ask questions about where we would live and where I would go to school and about my classmates. Usually, though, I tried not to ask too much, because her responses were so confusing that they actually tended to make me more scared than excited.

As the months and years passed, it seemed that the *campo* was fading from her thoughts. She sounded bored or distracted when I talked about people and happenings at home. A wall was beginning to separate us. While she seemed disinterested in our *campo*, I was just beginning to know it through my somewhat older eyes. Her thoughts were in *el Norte*, and I couldn't relate.

Over time, I became accustomed to my mother's absence, and her phone calls started becoming more of an obligation rather than something I looked forward to.

My *abuelita* and I slipped into our quiet routine of daily living. I helped her with the chores around the house before going to school. I was responsible for feeding the chickens, sweeping up the patio, and washing the dishes after meals. Our afternoons were filled with idle chatter with our neighbors and cleaning the house after lunch.

I often played with the kids who lived nearby. Sometimes I would go to the river with my best friend, Claribel, and we would play on its banks, imagining our lives as adults and acting out scenarios of caring for our homes and children in the *campo*, just as generations of women in our families had done. Occasionally, we would pack up pillowcases and go on picnics in the green rolling hills behind my house.

When Claribel was busy with chores, I enjoyed the errands my *abuelita* sent me on, picking up detergent or butter from our neighbor, who ran a small general store out of her house. I felt so grown up when my grandmother entrusted me with such responsibility. I enjoyed the comfort and regular, predictable nature of my life.

While our life in the *campo* seemed almost idyllic, there was also an undercurrent of uncertainty that penetrated our lives. More and more, the gossip around the *campo* focused on the gangs that had started terrorizing different communities around us. I wasn't sure exactly what was going on, but when I had heard words like *la Mara* and *pandillas,* I knew that the conversation had turned serious and it was my cue to leave the adults to their discussion.

In an effort to keep me safe, *abuelita* told me and Claribel to watch out for *personas sospechosas*, suspicious people, and to steer clear of situations that made us uncomfortable. Neither Claribel nor I really understood what a suspicious person was or how we could identify them. But we sensed that something was brewing in our *campo* and that we had to be aware.

Over the years, when I talked with *mamá*, she would tease me with the promise of being with her in *el Norte* and tell me how wonderful it would be when we were finally together. I wanted so much to be with her, but also found myself feeling guilty for my willingness to so easily leave my *abuelita* and the life we had together—she cared for me so lovingly, and *mamá*'s promises seemed to so easily pull me away.

Around my tenth birthday, I started having doubts that *mamá* would really send for me. Four years had passed since she left, and her weekly promises of taking me to *el Norte* started sounding more like cruel taunts or feeble attempts to win my love. Perhaps she sensed that she was slowly losing me. Each time she asked whether or not I wanted to go and live with her, I responded less enthusiastically.

Four years in the life a child is a long time. I was changing, and so was my idea of where *mamá* fit in my life. My *abuelita* had taken over in my day-to-day routine. She had filled the gap that my mother left four years before, and over time, my mother's place became less clear.

Then something changed. Shortly after I turned ten, I began imagining my reunion with *mami* on a daily basis. Each night, before drifting to sleep, I would imagine the day when we would be together again. Each night's reverie was slightly different, but every time, *mami* and I were reunited. Suddenly, more than anything, I wanted to be with her. She could have said she was taking me to hell, and I would have gone if it meant we were together.

Four

Esperanza

I called Luz as often as I could. It was always very painful to talk to her because each time we spoke it seemed that she was angrier and angrier with me. I wished she could have understood why I had to leave her.

Perhaps I could have explained to her about the threats of the *pandillas,* gangs, and the constant violence, and how staying in El Salvador would have meant certain death for both of us. Maybe I should have told her sooner what really happened to Diego so she would know that I didn't really have a choice about leaving.

I probably should have prepared her in some way for my departure. She was only six years old, and I knew she wouldn't understand if I told her I was leaving because of the violence that started plaguing our country over the last few years. But I should have given her more than the *mentirita,* the little lie, I told her. At the time, I thought it was the kindest way to leave. I thought that, if I just went away on a trip and then talked to her about it afterwards, things would be okay. I now realize that I didn't make it easier for her—lying to her was easier for *me.* My cowardice wasn't

27

fair to her, and it wasn't fair to my mother, who had to pick up the pieces I left behind.

I was certain that Luz would be fine with my mother and that, in a year or two, I would be able to send for her to come join me in *los Estados Unidos*. I never would have imagined it would take me *six years* to send for her. I didn't know what I was going to find in *el Norte*.

At that time, if you listened to people talk, *los Estados Unidos* was a dream come true. I thought that all I would have to do when I crossed the border was bend down and pick the dollar bills off of the ground. When friends called from *el Norte,* they made it sound like paradise. Perhaps they mentioned, here or there, that things were difficult, but when you constantly fear for your safety, you don't really want to hear that things everywhere are hard. I really thought I would just come here, start working, and in no time send for Luz.

Over the years, every time I spoke with Luz, I had a renewed hope and sense of urgency to send for her. When we'd talk on the phone, I tried to make her feel excited about coming. I missed her more than she could ever know.

I always carried a picture of her with me. It's from her first birthday. We didn't really have a party for her. We just had some cake and juice. But, thankfully, someone had taken the picture and given it to me. I looked at it every day and wondered what little changes were taking place in Luz.

When I left, she was six, and the picture still captured her essence. I wondered if, when I finally saw her again, I would recognize her. I wondered if this picture represented the person she was becoming.

It was only a matter of days until I would know for sure. I was so hopeful that the sacrifices I made to bring her to this country would finally pay off—they would have to pay off.

Making a life here, as an undocumented immigrant, has been difficult. I often feel like I have to live in the shadows. I work under the table and have limited access to healthcare. The bureaucracy around obtaining a driver's license makes transportation difficult, as well as finding and keeping good-paying work. I came here seeking safety and freedom for my family. Sometimes, though, it seems like I exchanged one uncertainty for another.

Instead of hiding from gangs in El Salvador, now I fear being deported back to those dangers. When I do participate in my new community, I feel so uncertain of my place because I can barely speak and understand English.

I left everything I knew and had in El Salvador, and came to this country following *el sueño Americano*, the

American dream. In some ways, it's been *una pesadilla,* a nightmare. Sometimes I question if it really is better for me to bring Luz here.

The truth is, while I'm worried about her coming, I can't leave her in a country where she is in constant danger.

My heart aches, every time I think that she is thousands of miles away from me and that I'm not raising her, but I know that when she gets here, if she can get through school and learn English, she can make something of herself. She can live the *true* American dream.

Five

Luz

Our trip to *el Norte* began uneventfully. We traveled in the back of the pickup to the nearest *pueblo*. Everyone rode in silence, watching the stunning landscape pass us by. As we left our community, I thought about how this was likely the last time I would see the deep green mountains that engulfed and protected my *campo*. I held on to the side of the pickup truck and examined the white clouds dotting the brilliant blue sky, picking out animal shapes and profiles of people in their ever-changing swirls. Occasionally, one of the old couple would murmur something to the other, or the mother would readjust her position in an attempt to sit more comfortably with her baby.

We shared an excitement, anticipating the journey ahead of us, yet we were also feeling cautious. There was no doubt that this journey could be perilous. Everyone had heard about people dying from heat exhaustion, exposure to the elements, or dehydration. I had even heard that some people would come across decomposing bodies along the way. We knew that murders and rapes were common, and we also knew not to mention those dangers now.

When we arrived in San Salvador, there was a flurry of activity, getting us transferred into several cars that were waiting in an abandoned parking lot. I was sad to separate from my fellow *campesinos*, as we had developed a sort of shared kinship. We had started our journey together, and that would connect us for much longer than the three hours we shared in back of the truck.

As we were divided up, the driver who had ferried us to the city got into some sort of confrontation with four or five other men who had arrived to take us to our destinations. They yelled frantically at each other, and their hands flew in all directions as they argued. It seemed that the argument was about which passengers would go in which vehicle.

I didn't understand what the problem was. I thought we were all going to the same destination, so why would it matter who went with whom? But I would find out soon enough just how much it mattered.

Maybe things would have turned out differently for me if the outcome of that argument had been different. It's surprising how one moment in time can so dramatically affect everything that follows.

The other passengers were separated into groups of two and sent to the various cars. I went by myself with one of the men from the parking lot. He was younger than the others and had striking blue-green eyes. He had dark skin and hair, but his eyes were so light that they reminded me of a cat's eyes or little blue-green marbles. He was the *coyote* responsible for getting me to our next destination.

I learned that *coyotes* are those—men, usually—who prey on the misfortune of others to make "dirty" money. They escort desperate immigrants across the border to *los Estados Unidos* and are responsible for getting them to their final destinations in *el Norte*

After separating into different cars, the migrants were to make their way to Mexico—in my case, by plane. From there, we would travel to the Mexico-US border, where we would meet up again. It sounded easy, and, indeed, getting to Mexico was fine. The green-eyed *coyote* and I took a plane to Mexico City, where he posed as my older brother and, with falsified documents, got us through airport checkpoints without any problem.

A few days after leaving the *campo*, we met up with the other passengers from the pickup truck somewhere in Mexico, just south of Texas. I had spent the last few nights at various abandoned houses that had been transformed to provide shelter for travelers like me—those on their way from one place to another, transients who left no record of their passing through.

Eventually, our group from the *campo* joined up with about ten to fifteen people who came from other parts of Central America. Listening to snippets of conversations, I heard that, among others, there was a couple from Guatemala, an older man from Honduras, and a Cuban man who was attempting to enter the United States via Central America.

It was such a relief to be reunited with the people from my *campo*. Even though we barely knew each other, knowing that they had made the same journey as I had made brought me comfort. I felt safer, knowing that I was with people who knew a little bit about me, and they helped me maintain my identity as a Salvadoran, as Luz. I realized then that we're not identified by who we are alone, but rather, who we are in relation to others. My *abuelita* used to say, *"Dime con quién andas, y te diré quien eres."* "Tell me with whom you walk, and I'll tell you who you are." She said this almost every time I brought a new friend over as a way of questioning me about the person's integrity. Today, as I joined the others from my *campo*, I thought about how the people I was, literally, walking with were defining who I

34

was. With these *campesinos* by my side, I felt like a whole person. At least for a little while.

The *coyotes* explained that we would walk as group until we reached the border. We would cross over into Texas and from there be ferried to our final destination, wherever that might be, in *los Estados Unidos.* In my case, I learned that I would be meeting my mother in a state called Maryland, near *la casa blanca,* where the president lives.

It was well after five in the afternoon when we finally set off for the perilous trek through the desert. My mother had warned me about this part of the journey and told me that it would be the most difficult.

The rocky terrain seemed endless as I searched the horizon for our destination, the border between Mexico and the United States. The *coyotes* pointed in the direction we were headed, and I was certain that, if I looked closely enough on the horizon, I could see the border that they had talked about. I imagined a finish line marking the end of Mexico and the beginning of the United States. Perhaps if I could see that mark, maybe the journey wouldn't be as bad as *mami* had told me it would be.

Instead, in every direction I looked, huge grey rocks started glowing red as the late afternoon sun reflected off of their surfaces. The rocky sand was pocked with short thorny shrubs, and as the sun moved lower along the horizon, the sky blazed with bright shades of pink and dark purples. I was simultaneously filled with awe at the beauty of the landscape and frightened by the never-ending immensity of it.

As we started walking, things didn't seem as bad as I had anticipated. The sun was lowering in the sky, and the afternoon heat had subsided. For about an hour, we walked steadily and with purpose. I even began to wonder what all the concern for the journey to *el Norte* was about, how people could die on this journey when I could see that it wasn't too difficult.

But as the hours went on and my legs ached, I started doubting my initial thoughts. My feet started hurting so much and the muscles in my calves and thighs began throbbing. Blisters had formed on my heels and on the balls of my feet, adding to the discomfort, making it even more difficult to walk.

The mother from the pickup was still carrying her baby. I looked toward her and wondered how she was doing it. I knew how uncomfortable I was, just walking for myself and carrying only my backpack. I wondered how on earth she could have carried that baby all this time. The little one occasionally fussed but was generally quiet. How was she feeding him? Would she have to stop to nurse him? What had she done, up until this point, to nourish him? Would the whole group stop to let her feed him? How her arms must have ached, carrying the child! I suddenly had a whole new appreciation for her journey.

And then I realized that she was doing what *my* mother didn't have the courage to do. This mother hadn't left her baby in El Salvador with his grandmother. Instead, she had made sacrifices by bringing him with her. Everyone had always told me that my mother was making sacrifices to make a better life for me. But not her own—she sacrificed *me* so that she could have a better life for herself!

This woman, walking next to me, was a *true* mother. She loved her child and knew that she wouldn't leave him to be raised by someone else so she could escape the despair of our country. Why couldn't my mother have known that?

I thought of *mami*, living the American dream over these last six years while I missed her, needed her, and yearned to be with her. Fury bubbled inside of me. I felt my face reddening and my hands beginning to tremble. A knot formed in my throat. I continued walking, silently, with an aching in my heart.

Well after the sun had set and after we had been walking by moonlight for quite some time, I heard someone call out, saying he was stopping to rest—the man who had been in the truck with me, the husband of the older couple dressed in their best clothes for this journey. We had been walking for at least five or six hours, and the effort was taking a toll on him and his wife. I looked back at them, the moon highlighting their faces, as they sat on a rock in the desert.

They were holding hands with each other as they rested. Their hands seemed to fit together effortlessly, as if they were two parts of the same body, a perfect mirror image. I could tell by the man's rugged face that he had spent countless years in the sun. He was probably one of so many who had worked his wiry body for hours in the fields, picking coffee or clearing land—doing work more suited to a beast of burden than a man.

But those times had passed. He probably hadn't worked that hard in a long time. This journey was exhausting him. I wondered if he had begun to ask what had happened to the strength of his youth. And I worried that he would not make it to his destination.

The mother of the baby stopped, too. The baby started whimpering a little, and she had beads of sweat on her upper lip and nose. The temperature had dropped considerably since we set off in the afternoon, and I was actually starting to feel a little chilly. The effort of carrying her child must have been exhausting and, even with the cooler temperatures she was sweating to keep cool.

A few others stopped, too. After so many hours, we were all so tired. I looked back at the small cluster forming around the rock. I looked ahead, to the rest of the group marching forward. The moon was shining down on us and, thanks to its light, we could see through the darkness. A few of the *coyotes* urged the group to move forward.

"It's safer to travel at night. The *policía* have a harder time finding us in the darkness. We must keep moving!"

It was unclear whether or not they were really concerned for our safety. Did they care at all if we made it to *el Norte?* Probably not, but they were guaranteed several thousand dollars for each person they brought on the trip. I doubted that they'd get paid if we didn't make it.

The *coyotes* started talking to one another about what they would do, now that they had two groups on their hands—one that had stopped, and another that pressed forward. But they had made this trip so many times, they were used to such situations. After less than a minute of discussion, two of the *coyotes,* the one with the green eyes and another one, stayed with those of us at the rock, and the others went ahead with the rest of the group.

I decided to stay back and rest with the older couple and the mother because my feet hurt so much. I didn't realize, when I left the *campo,* just how much I would be walking. When I had prepared for my trip, I had thought carefully about what I would wear on my journey. I had wanted to look nice when I arrived in the United States. I didn't want *mami* to think that my *abuelita* wasn't taking care of me.

My vanity, though, meant that I brought clothes that weren't very comfortable. My jeans, while they looked nice on me, were starting to feel too constrictive, and the button was rubbing against my abdomen. My shoes were the worst—I could feel the blisters on my feet and wished that I had heeded my grandmother's advice and brought something more appropriate for walking.

I sat down on the rock next to the nursing mother. I learned that her name was Maria and her baby's name was Diego.

"Diego! That was my father's name!" I said excitedly. I found out that the baby was five months old. He had a round face and thick, curly black hair that made him look older. He was dressed in a blue pajama-like jumper, and his little legs kicked about wildly from beneath his mother's arm. He seemed to be quite a sweet little baby, but I had started wondering how his mother could stand him, let alone tend to him, after such a long, excruciating walk. And this was just the beginning!

How many more days of walking would we have to endure?

"Let's stop here for the night," said the elderly lady. I could see that she was spent. Her eyes gave her away. They seemed more sunken than they did when we departed. Her skin looked more wrinkled, and the creases in her face seemed deeper and her cheeks more hollow.

Everyone agreed that this would be a good place to stop. There were some short trees nearby, and rocks that could provide some privacy. The elderly couple set up their meager blankets on the back side of their rock. I went with Diego's mother to a nearby tree, and we put down our blankets and bundled up in jackets to keep warm.

As each hour had passed since sunset, the temperature had fallen a degree or two. I was perplexed at how it had been so hot earlier in the day and how it now had become so cold that I had started shivering.

41

Diego's mother set him down on the blanket, and I could see the relief in her face as she was able to finally find reprieve from her delicate load. The baby sat and cooed for a few minutes. His mother lay down next to him and cuddled him up against her body. She lifted layers of jacket and shirts, offering her little baby her breast. He shook his head vigorously from side to side as he searched for the nipple. Finally, he found it and started filling his belly.

Watching Diego, I realized that I, too, was hungry. I hadn't eaten since around noon, a few hours before we set off. I thought of what I had in my backpack to eat, and then thought about how tired I was. Was I more hungry or tired? I decided that I needed sleep more than nourishment. Looking up at the moon as I lay in that desert wilderness, I thought about my a*buelita*. I felt comforted, knowing that she was seeing the same moon, even though we were now hundreds, maybe thousands, of miles apart. While studying the moon's craters and thinking of *abuelita*, I drifted to sleep.

Six

Esperanza

Oh my! When I finally saw Luz again, she took my breath away. My doubts about whether I would recognize her disappeared. I fell to my knees and wrapped my arms around her dirty jeans. Through my tears, I thanked God that she was standing in front of me. I couldn't believe the day had finally come!

Her hair was matted and she had a cut on her lip. Beneath her eyes, the dark circles showed more than the exhaustion that the trip across the desert had caused her.

Her face, although narrower and longer than when she was six was the same. But somehow she seemed different. Physically, as I had expected, she had changed, but now something else was different about her too. She had transformed even from the girl I had spoken to on the phone less than a month before.

Now, when she spoke, I sensed that something about her voice had changed, too. Before she had left the *campo* to come here, we spoke for at least an hour. I told her how proud I was of her and how I couldn't wait for her to come. I told her what to expect and to be very careful on

43

her trip here. She answered with excitement and anticipation. But when she spoke to me in the parking lot, something seemed different. Now I was wondering if, perhaps, her voice had lost its innocence.

Seven

Luz

I felt my lip split open as it got caught between my teeth and his hand, which was cupped over my mouth. I opened my eyes and saw the moon looking down at me. What was happening? I tried to move but quickly discovered that my arms were pinned firmly beneath his knees. He was straddling me—sitting on top of me—and had covered my mouth to muffle the sounds that he knew I would make when I awoke.

I jerked my head from side to side as hard as I could, trying to get loose, but that was useless. I started screaming, but with each sound I made, he tightened his legs around my sides, and then moved his hand to cover my nose. I couldn't breathe. If I didn't struggle, I could get little gasps of air into my nose and mouth through his thick leathery fingers. His hands smelled like smoke, alcohol and sweat.

He leaned down, toward my face, until his cheek was against mine.

"This will be much better for you if you don't struggle," he said, sitting up again to look at me.

Ever so slightly, he released his iron grip from my face. Without realizing it, I instinctively tried to wrestle free, and again, he grabbed my face, this time clamping my chin in the curve between his thumb and index finger. His thumb and other fingers were tightening, like a vise, around my face, squeezing my cheeks.

"I told you that this will work out better for you if you cooperate, *hija de puta*!" His hushed, raspy whisper lingered in my ear.

I tried to search around for baby Diego and his mother, both of whom had been next to me when I had fallen asleep. But his grip on my face made it impossible for me to look anywhere other than directly in front of me. All I could see was his shadowed face. The moon was behind him, and when he sat up to look at me, his head and curly hair blocked its light. A rim of light framed his head and his face was pure darkness, like the moon during a lunar eclipse. Just a short while ago, the moon's light had been guiding me through the desert, but now its light, around his body, was blinding me.

He lowered his head again next to mine and released me from his death grip. The stubble on his face scraped my cheek. I felt his chin press into my neck. When he started kissing me, I lowered my chin to my shoulder in an attempt to rebuff him.

Slowly he released my arms from under his knees, but then quickly grabbed them with one hand—he was so much bigger and stronger than I was. Still straddling me, he shifted my arms above my head. With his other hand, he lifted up my shirt and began grabbing my small, developing breasts. His groping hurt me and I tried moving away, to no avail.

He had started kissing my neck again, and then suddenly put his lips over mine and thrust his tongue into my mouth. I could taste the alcohol and cigarettes, and started to gag. I couldn't breathe. Again, I tried to move my head from side to side, and again, I couldn't escape.

It was just as he'd said—the more I struggled, the worse things were. When I moved, he tightened his whole body and constricted my movements even more. If I stayed still, his movements were less forceful and didn't hurt as much. In my naïveté, I thought that if I stayed still and didn't make a sound, maybe he would just kiss me and that would be it.

Just then, I felt his legs move. First he moved both of his knees on top of my thighs. He must have weighed five hundred pounds, because when I felt the weight on my legs, I thought my bones would break, it hurt so much. He then opened my legs by pushing one of his knees between my thighs. Even though I used all of my strength to try to keep my legs together, his weight and size made it easy for him to power through every ounce of effort I put forth.

Before I knew it, he had both of his knees between my legs, and then he started to move, rubbing against me. He still had his hand under my shirt, grabbing my chest while licking my face and moving his heavy body against mine. His foul odor permeated the air.

He abruptly took his hand out of my shirt and started unbuttoning his pants.

"Oh my God!" I thought, "Why is this happening!"

I started struggling again and almost managed to get one of my hands free. But when he felt me move, he clenched his whole body again. Then he moved his face back to my neck, and this time, sunk his teeth deep into my shoulder. I shrieked when the pain of his bite registered. And just as he had intended, I became compliant again. Every time I tried to struggle, he became more and more violent.

His hand moved back to his pants and he lowered them. He then reached for my pants and when he found the button undone, he slipped his hand into my panties.

"You were waiting for me to come to you, weren't you? *¡Maldita puta!*"

At that moment, I regretted having unbuttoned my pants before I went to sleep, but I had been getting so uncomfortable. When I felt him touching me, I imagined his stinking hands and dirty fingernails and wanted to jump out of my skin.

I could feel the tears falling down my face, but was unable to wipe them away. He moved his hand and then quickly entered me with his body. I thought this would kill me. With each movement, I felt my insides rip apart and my heart break into smaller and smaller pieces.

Eventually, he stopped. He let go of my hands and the weight of his body fell forcefully on top of me, forcing all the air out of my lungs, preventing me from inhaling. Unable to breathe, another wave of panic overcame me, and I tried to push him off of me but couldn't. Again, I realized that if I stopped struggling, then things would be better. I took small short breaths and was able to take air into my lungs.

He stayed on top and inside of me. Lifting his head and grabbing my face, he said that if I told anyone what we had just done, he would kill me and leave me rotting in the desert.

"What *we* had just done?" I thought to myself. *I* didn't do that! *That* wasn't my choice. He forced me to do this awful thing—he *made* me! I hadn't wanted this. My lip started to tremble when it occurred to me that perhaps I had somehow brought this on myself, that I had somehow encouraged him. When he saw my reaction, he smacked me across the face.

"*Mira, puta!* I told you that if you tell anyone about this, I will kill you and leave you here in the desert! You understand?"

He grabbed a gun that he had hidden away and pressed it against the temple of my head.

"*¿Entendés?*" he said again.

Trembling, I nodded that I understood. He moved toward my face again with the gun still pressed against my head and pressed his lips against mine, thrusting his tongue into my mouth again. Finally off of me, he buttoned up his pants and walked away. As he turned toward the moon, I saw his face in profile and realized that he was the *coyote* that had been on the plane with me, the one with the green eyes, the one that had posed as my older brother.

Once he was gone, I looked up at the moon shining brightly down on me. I thought about my *abuelita* being under that same moon. Earlier, when I had fallen asleep, this thought had brought me comfort. But now it was torturing me, knowing that somehow the moon had witnessed what had just happened and was reflecting it back to my grandmother.

Eight

Esperanza

It had been nearly three weeks since Luz had left our *campo* in El Salvador. After crossing the border in Texas, she spent several days moving within the United States until she arrived at our home in Maryland.

When she first arrived and saw our apartment for the first time, I was excited to show her how everything was different, here. I tried to show her around and make her feel comfortable. I had cooked *pupusas* for her, and rice and beans and salad, and almost everything I could think of to make her feel at home. The journey to *el Norte* is long and hard, and I just wanted to be able to fill her belly after such a torturous experience. After so many years, I longed to be the one to nourish her. It made me feel good to think that finally she would be full with food that I had cooked.

Hoping that she would eat ravenously, devouring the meal that I had prepared, I sat at the table, chin in hand, watching her with anticipation. I couldn't wait to see her face when she was confronted with all of the abundance of her new life. Instead, I was surprised and somewhat disappointed when she ate only one *pupusa* and then asked to be excused.

When Luz asked to take a shower, I took her to the bathroom so she could get cleaned up. I showed her how to use the faucet and tap, and suggested that maybe she'd want to take a bath with hot water and soak for a while. She said she didn't want to.

Handing her a fresh new towel, I adjusted the water's temperature and expected her to start getting undressed to shower. She used to take showers with me when she was little, and I hadn't even imagined that she wouldn't feel comfortable getting undressed in front of me. But instead, she stood awkwardly looking at me, waiting for me to leave. I gave her the space she obviously wanted and went to the bedroom.

When she came out of the shower with the towel wrapped around her, I saw a crescent-shaped mark on her shoulder. Fear rose and caught in my throat. I didn't know what had happened to her, and I was afraid to ask. Whatever it was, I felt responsible.

I walked over to my daughter and put my hands on her shoulders. With my thumb, I rubbed the spot where the mark was. When I tried to look her in the eyes, asking if everything was okay, she wouldn't look at me. She hung her head low, and I only realized that she was crying when a teardrop landed on my foot. I pulled her close to me to give her another hug, but she fell to the floor, sobbing.

Nine

Luz

For Salvadoran *campesinas*, the journey to the United States isn't about boarding a plane and arriving to the welcoming smiles and hugs of extended relatives. Rather, our journeys are ones of brutal, forced entry into a country that seems to close its doors at every turn.

The day I left my *abuelita*'s house, I was a naïve twelve-year-old, trusting and unaware of how awful human beings can be to one another. How could I have known any differently? Up until then, the defining moment of my life was when I realized that my mother had left our *campo* for good, for *el Norte*. That tore me apart.

But what happened in that desert not only physically tore me apart, but also ripped away my sense of being. Only a shell of the Luz who left the *campo* remained.

After the *coyote* left me on the ground, I rolled over to my side and pulled my pants back on. Then I buttoned them up, curled up into a ball on the ground, and cried. Hiding my face in my jacket, I wept for a while. When I looked up, I noticed that the sky was changing as the sun started emerging over the horizon.

Slowly I stood up, unsteady on my feet, and took a few halting steps. The pain between my legs as I walked was unbearable. My scrambled insides felt like they would fall out of me. I felt the urge to go to the bathroom but was scared to see what was causing me so much pain.

Walking some more, I looked around for the others who had also stopped for the night and saw them a little bit away, still sleeping. My attacker had fallen asleep again, next to the other *coyote*, and the two were snoring loudly.

Baby Diego and his mother were over in another area, and they, too, were sleeping. Why wasn't she next to me anymore? Why had she left me? Did the *coyote* make her leave? Had she left me alone because Diego had started crying and she didn't want his cries to wake me? Why hadn't she stayed to protect me? I clenched my teeth, in an effort to keep from bursting into tears again.

I walked slowly and carefully to a large rock a short distance away. I had to pee and face the disaster between my legs. Behind the rock, out of sight of the others, I opened my pants and slowly slipped them down to my knees. There was blood on my thighs and my underwear were stained with blood and a milky substance that I guess the *coyote* had left inside of me.

Quickly, I lifted my pants and went back to get my backpack. I gathered all of my stuff together, shoved my flimsy blanket into my backpack, and retreated behind the rock. I lowered my pants again and this time slipped them off to clean myself with some drinking water I had in my bag.

The water was cold from the frigid night temperatures, and its coldness was chilling on my skin. Although I was so sore from what the *coyote* had brutally done to me, the cold was a welcome yet temporary anesthetic.

Using more of the water, I attempted to wash my face. I felt the dried blood on my lip and did my best to remove all evidence of it. Pushing my shirt off of my shoulder, I examined where he had bitten me. The skin was broken, and I could see the crescent-shaped outline of his teeth and a bruise starting to form under the skin.

I stood up, leaned against the rock, and inhaled deeply. The tears came back, and I cried silently for a few minutes. "No!" I told myself, "I'm fine," and I reached into my backpack for a change of clothes. I gingerly slid on a clean pair of underwear and pants.

I wondered what I should do with my soiled clothes. I couldn't take them to my mother's house. I could never tell her what happened. Not only would the *coyote* kill me, but also, what would my mother think of me? Would she think that *I* had caused this—I wondered if, maybe, I had.

I buried the dirty clothes a little beyond the rock that I had been leaning against. By leaving them in the desert, perhaps the whole experience would stay there, buried forever.

As I waited for everyone else to wake up, I lay on the ground and looked up to the sky; the brilliant shades of pink, orange and purple were so beautiful as the sun moved higher in the sky. Finally, I heard Diego start to stir. His mother nursed him.

Ten

Esperanza

After Diego left the *campo*, the days seemed interminable until our baby was finally born. Her arrival was as joyous as I had imagined. She came out of me and was placed on top of my stomach. When I looked down at her and she looked knowingly back at me, she had a look in her eyes. It was as if she had chosen me from above to be her mother and for the first time saw my face. Perhaps the universe had sent her to me and was telling me, in that instant, that the whole reason for my life was to raise this child.

I'm not sure how my sixteen-year-old mind was able to comprehend it, but I think it was that instant that she looked at me—that one brief second before she took her first breath and started screaming, that instant between life and death, when it wasn't clear whether or not she would breathe—that revealed the gravity of my new role as her mother. It was a brief, almost imperceptible moment, but I knew then that everything had changed.

A few weeks after Luz was born, I took her to the city to meet her father for the first time. Everyone in the *campo* told me that she was too young to withstand a bus ride through the mountains and that I shouldn't go. But I couldn't stand that Diego hadn't yet seen his daughter. He had been in the city for a few months and couldn't go back to the *campo* to meet Luz because he would lose his job if he took time off work. If that happened, he wouldn't be able to support our new family. He had just found a place for us to live and was ready to bring us to the city to be with him for good.

It was early afternoon, and the sun had already started beating down on the cream-colored tiles that paved the driveway of the bus terminal. The blazing heat was relentless as I held Luz, waiting for Diego to pick us up. I didn't know where to go, so we stood off to the side of the terminal while other passengers frantically moved around us.

Finally, I saw him. He hadn't yet seen me, and I watched his face, waiting for the moment when he first spotted me through the crowd and the flash of recognition softened his expression. A smile exposed his straight, white teeth and his eyes darted around, looking frantically for his daughter. When he finally saw Luz, tears welled up in his eyes as he lifted her up and wrapped his arms around her little body. He pulled her close to his chest, her head beneath his chin, and his arms cradled and enveloped her. Even among the commotion of the bus stop, it was as if time stood still as father and daughter met for the first time.

After a few moments, Diego rested Luz in his left arm and looked down at her perfect, delicate face. Using his right hand, he traced the outline of her closed eyes and the gentle curve of her nose. Then he leaned his head down to her and kissed her on the forehead. Holding her with the ease and confidence of someone born to be father, I wondered how this role came so naturally to him.

He tightly closed his eyes as he pressed her against his cheek, keeping her there for at least a minute, as if trying to attach his soul to hers. He then pulled me close to him, and the three of us stood there, embracing one another, trying to make up for the months that we had been apart.

Other passengers in the bus station busily moved around us, as if we were not there. I felt enveloped in a protected bubble; everything around us kept going, but time stood still in this sacred space. I knew, there and then, that Diego, Luz, and I were truly a family. No matter what, all three of us were united and would always be together. The love that we shared at that moment transcended anything that I had ever known.

I'm not sure how long we stood there, but as Diego loosened his embrace, he pulled away and looked me up and down. Smiling the biggest grin I had ever seen him give, he wiped the tears from his eyes. He told me that I had done wonderful work, bringing his daughter into the world, and that he was so proud to have his family with him.

Diego brought us to the restaurant where he worked and sat us down at a table. He told the other employees at the restaurant to come out and meet the two wonderful women in his life. Taking Luz from my arms, he beamed while his coworkers complimented his beautiful daughter, his *princesa*.

The restaurant owner offered us a meal of *sopa de pollo* to celebrate the beginning of our new life in the city together. Everyone took turns passing Luz around and admiring her. She slept through the excitement, as only a newborn can. I felt so happy to finally be with Diego again and felt certain of our future together. Looking at him as he talked to everyone in the restaurant, I felt that I was the luckiest person in the world.

Eleven

Luz

As I listened to baby Diego nurse, I relived, in my mind, the horror of what had just happened. I couldn't believe what the *coyote* had done to me. Placing my hand on my abdomen, below my navel, I tried to soothe my aching insides. They felt as if they had been swirled together in a blender and then ripped out. The soft pressure of my hand relieved some of the torment within me.

I couldn't help but wonder how I had ended up in this situation. What had I done to deserve this? Had I provoked the *coyote*? Could I have done something differently that would have prevented this? Could someone have protected me from this?

Listening to baby Diego, I thought of the other Diego in my life, the one I had always wished would protect me—the one who didn't live long enough to protect me.

Mami had told me the story of my *papi's* death only one time, but then we never spoke of it again. She told me about it a few years after she left, while we were speaking on the phone one day, when she had called from *el Norte*. It was one of the conversations during which I had been particularly obstinate.

As usual, she was ignoring my petulance, doing her best to make small talk about what I had done that day at school. But I was having none of it and just gave her a curt, one-word response. She continued speaking calmly and sweetly.

Finally, I told her I had to go, and I hung up the phone as she was saying good-bye. As I left my neighbor's house, where I often took her calls, the phone rang. Curious as to who was calling, I slowed my pace and listened as my neighbor answered. Crossing the front door's threshold, I heard my neighbor say my name.

"*Luz, te llama tu mamá.*"

I looked over my shoulder and scrunched up my face to ask why she was calling again. Then I walked slowly back to the phone—I really wasn't interested in speaking with my mother again, but I didn't want to be rude to my neighbor, who was gracious enough to allow me to use the phone. Smiling sweetly, disguising the rudeness with which I was prepared to answer my mother, I gently took the phone. I put the receiver to my ear, turning away so my neighbor wouldn't hear how harshly I would respond to my mother.

"*¿Qué?*" I huffed at her.

I heard my mother speaking very quietly and calmly, in a very measured tone.

"Luz, I am going to tell you something. This is something very difficult for me to say, and I need you to listen."

Realizing that she was about to tell me something very important, but not yet willing to give up the disagreeable attitude, I responded with a very surly "*¿Qué?*"

She continued, very slowly, as she told me the story of how my father had been murdered.

"*Asasinado,*" I whispered to myself.

My mother told me about coming to the city shortly after my birth to start a new life as a family. She told me how, when my father saw me for the first time, he held me and looked at me as if he had loved me his whole life. I wondered what that must have looked like.

There is only one picture of my father that I remember seeing, and I could barely make out his face. With that image in my mind's eye, I tried imagining how he must have looked at me, that day. I wondered if anyone would ever look at me that way again. Would I ever look at anyone in that way?

She told me that the three of us, out together for the first time, went to the small restaurant where my *papi* worked so he could show me off to his new city friends—he was so proud to be a father.

I never really understood how he could have been proud of a little baby. After all, I had not done anything to make him proud. But whenever *mamá* talked about him, she would say how much he loved me and how proud he was of me.

Whenever I had asked about him, she had told me that he died in an accident. I had assumed that she meant a car accident, and never really pressed her on it because each time she said it, her whole demeanor changed. I knew it upset her, so I stopped asking because I didn't want to make her cry. It was scary for me to see *mami* cry, and I would do anything to keep her from crying. So I grew used to living with not knowing what had actually happened to my father.

As she told me the story of his murder, she painted a strangely beautiful picture leading up to his death. It started as a story of hope and happiness. If I hadn't known that it would end with my father's death, I would have assumed the ending would have been very different. She separated the day into two separate events—one of happiness and joy and the other of awful, heartbreaking tragedy—incongruous, not connecting as one.

Twelve

Esperanza

The restaurant where Diego worked was on the southeast corner of the city's central plaza. On one side, large glass windows looked out on the street and across to the greenery of the plaza. Couples held hands as they strolled, and children happily rode their bikes. Through the opposite windows, patrons could see small, brightly colored, wood-slat homes across the main boulevard. I distinctly remembered a bright blue home with pink trim around its door and windows. It caught my eye because it was just as my house had been painted when I was a child

I can recall every detail of that day so vividly—the peeling yellow paint on the restaurant walls, walls that were once so beautiful, the owner's pride. Dirty finger- and handprint smudges now stained the doorjamb from years of customers resting their hands on the wall as they exited the front door.

Diego cradled Luz so lovingly in his arms as we walked through that door. He had the biggest smile on his face as he introduced her to the staff. We sat down at a table for four that was covered in a clear plastic tablecloth that was slightly sticky from being wiped down but not really clean.

I turned and smiled at Diego, taking him in anew after our time apart. He was freshly showered and smelled of clean clothes and *cuaba* soap. He had gone from a thin, lanky teenager to a strong man with a sharp jawline and strong arms defined by muscles. I was proud that I was in love with such a handsome man and that he was in love with me. I wondered if, perhaps, he had noticed any change in me, too, and planned to ask him about it later that night.

I watched with pride as he maneuvered Luz, tending to her as if he were an experienced father—no evidence that he was new to being a parent. Any of my doubts about him, and us, disappeared.

Moving Luz from the crook of his arm to his shoulder, Diego leaned his cheek against the top of her tiny little head, inhaling the sweet smell of her wispy dark hair that lightly tickled his face. It was as if he couldn't get enough of her. He wanted to make up for the time he had lost—the weeks apart had felt like ages to him.

These moments at the table were magical, and I was jubilant. Our family was united. It was such a miracle, and the rest of the world continued around us, oblivious.

Then the awful thing happened; the moment I was pulled away from our beautiful idyll. The restaurant door opened and its bell jingled, pulling my attention away from Diego and Luz. Looking up and away, I saw a man, quickly and purposefully, walk over to Diego. His movements were fast and intentional, but I saw everything in clear detail, as if it had happened in slow motion.

The man had tattoos on his face and arms, his white short-sleeved shirt hugged his chest, and his head was cleanly shaved. He approached Diego from behind. Diego was oblivious to what was unfolding behind him, looking sideways at Luz as he continued basking in his newfound joys of fatherhood. I thought that perhaps Diego and the bald man in white knew each other.

Suddenly, I heard a deafening crack, a loud pop. In an instant, the man's clean white T-shirt was sprayed with red droplets. Diego fell to the floor, still holding Luz in his arms. The man in white turned and pointed the gun, his hands shaking, at the restaurant owner, who was standing behind the counter.

"This is your warning," he said, his voice wavering. "The next time I have to come here, this will be you."

He pointed his gun back down at Diego on the floor. I couldn't understand what was happening and wondered if the man realized that Diego had Luz in his arms.

I heard Luz's muffled cry coming from beneath Diego's limp, still body. I watched as blood pooled below his head, and then I heard him take his final breath – his soul leaving his body as he exhaled for the last time.

Touching my face—it had become wet—I realized that I, too, had droplets of Diego's blood on me. Somehow, I managed to stand up and look at the horrifying scene on the floor, not knowing what to do.

The man in the white T-shirt scurried out of the restaurant. I watched him, through the window, as he put his gun in his pants and smoothed down his shirt. As quickly as he entered, he was gone.

It took some time before I could think clearly enough to gather up Luz from under the weight of Diego's lifeless body. I had to push him off of her, rolling him away from me. I sat on the floor next to him, holding my baby in my arms. She wailed, and I heard myself sobbing as I patted Diego's head and tried to clean the blood off of him.

The whole incident happened in less than a minute.

Thirteen

Luz

I remember listening to *mami* intently, gripping the phone tightly as I heard what had happened to *papi*, to us.

As I listened, I simultaneously felt joy and rage about what I was hearing—imagining a wonderful life that could have been, but was cut short.

Mamá told me that my father had died quickly, after the bullet entered his skull, but that she felt that if she stayed by his side, she could somehow keep him with her until help arrived. As she sat on the floor of the restaurant, her bloodied baby in her arms, all she could think of was cleaning the blood spatter off of my father and me. She knew it didn't make any sense to clean us off in that moment, but it was the only thing that seemed within her ability to do.

As she spoke, I couldn't help but wonder if she really knew that she was talking to me, her daughter. She was talking as if I were her friend. I felt a little embarrassed by what she was saying, like maybe I was hearing some things, some details, I shouldn't be hearing.

Afraid to ask, but equally afraid not to, I finally squeaked out a question.

"Who killed him?"

In a way, it didn't really matter. It mattered that my mother wanted justice for her husband's murder, for the shattered future of her baby's father, for the life she could no longer have. But it didn't matter because it wouldn't bring my father back. He had been dead for so long, and I had lived my first ten years without him, so how could knowing who had done this make a difference for me?

My mother hesitated for a moment and then whispered, "*La Mara.*" I was silent on the other end of the phone.

As she explained, it became clear, and scary. She told me that my father had left the *campo* to go to the city and started working at the restaurant. Gangs had been active in the city for years, one of the many unforeseen but most deadly consequences of our country's twelve-years-long civil war. The gangs hadn't started charging *la renta* until very recently. *La renta* was just that—a rent charged to local merchants, doctors, bus drivers, *anyone* that could be harassed into paying a small amount each day to guarantee their safety.

At first, gang members told people that *la renta* would keep them safe from rival gangs who were trying to encroach on their territory. But very soon, they realized that *la renta* was actually keeping them safe from the very people charging them. The man who killed my father was telling the owner of the restaurant that, if he didn't continue to pay *la renta*, he, too, would meet the same fate. My father had lost his life to set an example.

"La Mara killed your father," my mother said again. "You see, Luz, what I wanted for you was something different. I dreamt of making a life with you and your father and raising you in our country, as a family. I didn't leave you with your grandmother so I could come to *el Norte* to escape my responsibilities. I came here because I had no other choice. The only thing I could do to ensure your safety was to come here. I didn't leave you because I don't love you; I left you because I do.

"I know you can't understand that right now, but maybe you'll remember this, and one day you'll understand that everything I've done was for you. So when you get angry with me and don't want to talk, I understand that you're hurting and that you want something different. But I need you to know that I did the very best I could for you, given the impossible circumstances of our lives and the unlivable conditions in our country."

I stood in silence, holding the phone, listening to her try to catch her breath while trying to hide the pain in her voice. My heart ached for how I had treated her that day, and all of the days before.

* * * *

I remembered this story as I lay in the dirt and watched the sun rise over the horizon. I felt the stinging between my legs as I was pulled back into reality. I heard a stirring and remembered the baby that was traveling with me—Diego. It was no coincidence that Diego was my traveling companion. My father was with me. He knew what happened. Would he still feel proud of me? Was he here, protecting me in some way after all?

Fourteen

Esperanza

As Luz sobbed at my feet, I fell to the floor next to her. Wrapping my arms around her shoulders, I told her that I loved her and that everything would be okay. But with each word I spoke, her crying became more and more intense, and I found myself crying along with her.

She wouldn't speak to me, so I rocked her in my arms and pulled her onto my lap, stroking her wet hair. I gently kissed her forehead. She was inconsolable, and I didn't know why, and I didn't know how to help her. All I could do was hold her in my arms.

After some time, her wails changed from hysterical howls to soft whimpering, as she started calming down. I lightly rocked her, as I did when she was a baby. More than thirty minutes passed before I took her chin in my hand and moved her head so I could see her face. She stared back at me with her glassy, bloodshot, tear-filled eyes. It broke my heart to look into them.

Much later, I took Luz to our bed. She curled up into a ball and hid her face beneath her pillow. A few moments later, she fell into a tortured sleep. Each time her breathing slowed down, when sleep finally set in, she'd startle awake. And with each awakening, she'd begin whimpering until exhaustion would once again overtake her. This happened repeatedly over the next few hours, as she struggled to find rest.

As I watched her, wishing that I could do something to help her, I looked at the soft, new sheets that she was sleeping on. I had bought them in anticipation of her arrival. I was so excited to have her with me again and had wanted to make this space feel like home for her. As I prepared our room, I imagined that we would laugh and play, as we had when she little. Of course, I knew she was older, but I was certain that things couldn't have changed that much. I remembered those sweet moments we shared before I left. I was so hopeful for our future in this new country.

I had made up the bed, imagining how nice it would feel for her to lie down on a fresh sheets after her long journey. I remembered lying down for the first time after arriving in *el Norte*. Feelings of relief, pride, joy, and uncertainty came over me when I finally had a moment to realize what I had just accomplished by getting here. That first night, after so many struggles, when you finally take in that you are starting a new, safe life in *los Estados Unidos*—

you're filled with so many emotions that seem impossible to experience all at once.

I had imagined the emotions that Luz might feel when her head hit the pillow on her first night. But I had not imagined that things would turn out so differently.

After watching Luz for a while longer, I slipped into bed next to her. I heard her sniffling, each time she jolted awake. I could tell she was trying to be silent and not let her emotions out. At one point, I reached over and touched her shoulder in an attempt to comfort her. But instead of feeling comforted, every muscle in her body tightened, and she went perfectly still.

When I felt her body constrict, I said her name, barely audibly, but hoping that she would turn to me. I wanted to talk to her but was too afraid to ask her what had happened. I was too afraid to know the answer.

I wanted to comfort her; it had been too long, since I had done that. But now she seemed like a stranger, lying next to me. Time and distance had been cruel. I wanted to make right whatever had gone wrong, but she wouldn't let me in.

Eventually, Luz relaxed some, easing into the space next to me. A short time later, I heard her draw in long, regular breaths and knew that the sleep that had eluded her for much of the night had finally set in.

I lay next to her in the dark, my mind racing, listening to her breathing, her sudden movements, and her soft grunts. I wondered what images were taking hold beneath her eyes as they rapidly moved back and forth under her closed lids. Was she dreaming about her grandmother back home? Her life before I left? Was she reliving her journey to *el Norte*? Were her dreams of sweet innocence, or was a nightmare unfolding?

The moon was nearly full that night, and my eyes followed a soft moonbeam as it illuminated Luz's gentle features. I sat up to examine her more closely. Looking at her beautiful face, for a moment I saw the little girl who I had left in the *campo* so many years ago. She was growing into a lovely young woman. I could see Diego in the outline of her nose and her thick eyebrows, and I saw myself in her high cheeks and her full lips—what a beautiful combination of Diego and me.

I wondered if Diego knew how lovely our daughter was. Did he look down from heaven or wherever he was and see what he had left on earth? I smiled at the thought and wondered if maybe he was the moonbeam shining down on her, looking upon us. I hearkened back to our all-too-brief time together and took comfort in thinking maybe he was with us now, when we needed him. Tears welled in my eyes. I thought about the life we could have had and considered the life unfolding before me.

When I sent for Luz, I knew that there would be danger lurking at every turn on her journey to *el Norte*, especially for a twelve-year-old girl. I had heard stories and seen with my own eyes what could happen—I had lived some of those stories myself. But I also knew that leaving her in El Salvador would be so much worse than the *possibility* of what might happen on the journey. I yearned for her to tell me what had happened. I hoped her story would not be too awful. Please let it not be too awful.

Fifteen

Luz

Just a few weeks after arriving in *el Norte,* I started seventh grade in my new school. I had arrived in early October, so this wasn't the first day for my classmates. All of the other kids already knew each other, and I would be starting behind everyone, all by myself. When I was in the *campo,* I had looked forward to going to school in *los Estados Unidos.* The thought of learning a new language was exciting, and Claribel and I used to practice what little we knew of English from time to time. The reality of it terrified me.

Mami sent me to the bus stop by myself. I waited for the bus on the corner near our apartment. Looking back toward my new home, I saw my mother peeking through the curtains, watching me from a distance. When she saw me, she quickly moved away, and the tattered curtain covering our kitchen window fell back into place. I wished that she would come with me to the bus stop, but she told me that it was better that I go by myself. She said it would make me stronger and more open to making new friends.

I didn't have the energy to convince her otherwise and didn't know how I could make her understand what I needed. My *abuelita* would have known and would have come with me.

The other kids at the bus stop mostly ignored me. Occasionally they said something to me in what seemed like a mix of Spanish and English. I was not used to this way of speaking and had a hard time understanding anything they said. It sounded like they had marbles in their mouths. All I could do was smile nervously at them.

The longer I stood there, the faster my heart pounded, and I thought it would beat right out of my chest. My palms were sweating and I started to feel tightness in my head. I tried calming myself with thoughts of my grandmother back at our house in our *campo*. Imagining her in the kitchen, tidying up after breakfast, brought me comfort. I wished she were here. I would have given anything in the world to have her by my side.

As a wave of nausea came over me, I thought I was going to pass out. Luckily, at that moment, the giant, orange school bus came hurtling down the road. It stopped and its doors swung open violently. All the kids started filing onto the bus. I lined up behind them and waited for my turn to climb the steep green stairs.

While I waited, I looked back at our apartment and saw my mom's face looking sullenly through the glass at me. She put her hand up and pressed it against the window. I looked back at the bus and felt a lump moving into my throat, tears starting to blur my vision. I wiped my eyes before the tears fell down my cheek. Will they ever stop falling?

As I looked back at the window, I saw the curtain rustle back to place. My mother had left her lookout. Again, she left me just when I needed her.

The bus had a strange smell of exhaust, sweat, and plastic. We didn't have school buses like this in the *campo*. There, everyone walked to school, even kids who lived far away. The heavyset woman driving the bus had curly orange hair and a mole on her cheek. She barked orders at the kids, I guess, telling them to take their seats. Everyone seemed to know where to go and found a spot to sit. But I didn't know where I was supposed to sit. There was an empty seat right behind the bus driver, and I sat there by myself.

As the other students talked with each other, the bus maneuvered loudly through the streets, stopping at different street corners to pick up more kids. I leaned forward in my seat and rested my head against the partition between the bus driver's seat and my own. My tears flowed freely for a few moments.

After the longest ten minutes I could have imagined, we arrived at the school. It was a huge brick building with lots of windows and, oh my God, *so* many kids. Looking down from the bus window, the students, in their matching uniform shirts, looked like thousands of ants scurrying around as they waited to enter the building. I couldn't believe that there were really that many kids at one school.

Fear sunk in, paralyzing me. I wasn't sure that I would be able to move myself from my seat. As the other kids filed off of the bus, I stared through the window at the swarm of students waiting to go inside. How on earth would I know where to go? I held my stomach and put my other hand to my mouth, certain that I would vomit.

I heard the bus driver yell something at me, and I looked up at the front of the bus and saw her reflection in the long mirror against the windshield. She had strange green eyes and big yellow teeth. Curling her lips, she shouted.

"You speaka da Ingles?"

I didn't understand the exact words she growled at me, but her feelings toward me were undeniable. I looked around for help, realizing again that everyone else had left the bus and that I would have to as well.

I managed to rise and walk down the deep bus steps until I felt my feet on the asphalt parking lot. The bus driver slammed shut the doors behind me, spewing some spiteful last words. The bus's tires squealed as she sped away.

Looking around for some clue as to what to do, I heard someone yelling, "Lucy, Lucy!" It was the counselor who had helped me enroll in school a few days earlier. He had called me Lucy the day I came with my mom to register, and I guess he thought that was my name.

He waved at me and had a big grin on his face as he approached. His kind, round face and soft voice made me feel a little better, but somehow his kindness also made me long for the comfort of something more familiar. I felt my chin start to tremble. I was becoming used to this sensation. I hoped that he wouldn't notice how scared I was.

He put his arm around my shoulder and guided me through the mass of students. For an instant, with the counselor's hand leading me into the building and down the hall, I wondered if a father's comfort would have felt like that. If my *papi* were with me, leading the way, maybe I would have felt safer.

The noise and commotion terrified me. Every fiber of my being yearned to run away. But where would I go? The bus had disoriented me, and I knew of nowhere to go. While I allowed the counselor to guide me through the maze, I couldn't wait until the school day ended.

The guidance counselor sat me down in a classroom, and my academic career in *los Estados Unidos* was underway. Students got up from their seats and yelled at each other. The teacher hollered at them, but the kids continued, ignoring the teacher's pleas.

At one point, two kids next to me started hitting each other, and pretty soon they were wrestling. They fell into my desk, and before I knew what was going on, I was knocked out of my seat. The teacher sat me up and sent the two boys out of the room. A girl next to me looked over apologetically and said something. I didn't understand her, so I quickly averted my eyes and looked down at my desk. She seemed nice, but I was terrified by the attention. I sensed that she was compassionate, and for that I was grateful.

Eventually, the teacher gained a little bit of control and the class settled down some. The teacher spoke in English, and her garbled words and squeaky voice intensified my headache.

My school in the *campo* was so different from what I was experiencing here. I had attended the same school since I started, when I was six years old. If I hadn't come to *El Norte*, I would have continued through eighth grade in the same building, with fewer than one hundred students in all, and I knew almost all of them by name. I think that, at this new school, I had seen one hundred kids in my first ten minutes.

I wondered how I would ever understand this crazy new school, this strange language, these rambunctious kids, these new teachers, and all of the commotion. It overwhelmed me. I sat in my first class in *el Norte* and rubbed my eyes, resting the heel of my hands in my eye-sockets, my fingers lingering along my hairline. I wished I could have stayed like that forever. I wished I could have disappeared.

Suddenly a loud horn-like tone sounded, and all of the kids started scurrying around and then left the room. I looked around, confused. The girl who had spoken to me earlier guided me up to the teacher and then left the room.

"*Ay Dios!* What now?" I thought to myself.

The teacher took me back to my desk and shuffled through some of the papers I had been given and asked me something. I wasn't sure what she wanted.

"*No entiendo.*" I replied—the only thing I could say.

Looking at her blankly and sort of shrugging my shoulders, I could feel that now-familiar knot rising into my throat. She mumbled under her breath as she continued searching for some unknown document. After shuffling more papers around, she found what she was looking for.

Handing me the papers that had been on my desk and grabbing my elbow, she hurriedly pushed me toward the door. I prayed that her impatience would force her to send me home. That didn't happen. Instead, she grabbed another student in the hallway and showed her my papers. Before I knew what was happening, the girl was pushing me through the mass of students in the hallway, guiding me into another classroom.

"*Me llamo Marisol. ¿Como te llamas?*" she said, once we arrived. "My name is Marisol. What's your name?"

I must have looked at her blankly, because she asked me again what my name was. I replied that my name was Luz. She smiled a perfect grin, with straight white teeth and kind, sweet eyes, and for the first time that day, I thought maybe I'd make it through.

Sixteen

Esperanza

Our lives started gaining some sense of normalcy. We would wake up early and have breakfast together, then I'd go to work and Luz would go to school. She would get home before me in the afternoons and sometimes prepare dinner for us. I often got home around five or six o'clock, and we'd spend the evenings together, usually watching TV or going to the stores nearby to look around.

At first, things seemed to be okay. I was trying to rebuild our relationship after so many years apart. But it was so hard to get through to Luz. She was withdrawn, and whenever I thought she was starting to come around, she would close back up again. I so hoped that time would heal whatever she was feeling.

One day, about three months after Luz arrived, I received a call from the school, from Luz's English teacher. I went outside of the house I was cleaning to hear her more clearly. Two teachers were calling, actually—one spoke English and the other interpreted into heavily accented Spanish.

Apparently, Luz seemed distant and withdrawn. The teacher had noticed it early on, but knew it was typical of students who had just immigrated, as they adjusted to their new schools and the new culture. She was concerned, though, because Luz didn't seem to be coming around. Usually, by this point, she said, students made friends and started feeling more comfortable at school. She was also concerned because Luz was missing so many days of school.

"What?" I thought to myself. Luz hadn't missed any school. I was stunned. Was this teacher talking about *my* Luz? Could she have mixed her up with someone else? I knew that Luz went to school every day. Other than one day, when she was sick and stayed home, I watched her get ready for school and walk to the bus stop. Luz should have had nearly perfect attendance. But I didn't let the teacher know that I had no idea what she was talking about.

As she continued, my heart started racing as I feared what Luz might be doing when she wasn't in school. I remembered the stories I had heard and imagined her running around with boys from the high school, or smoking cigarettes, or drinking, or doing drugs by the creek. I imagined her with older kids in the apartment complex and having sex at those "parties" the kids went to when they skipped school. I thought about the kids who had recently gone missing and wondered if their parents had received similar calls prior to them disappearing.

The teacher continued talking, but all I could think of was rushing home to find out what was happening. I no longer understood what she was saying. My mind was racing. I was angry and scared and needed to find out what was going on with Luz.

After ending the call, I sat down on the front steps of the house. I needed a moment to take in what I had just heard. I inhaled a deep breath and let it out with a long sigh, then did it again. I tried to calm down, but started feeling dizzy. My ears felt like they were closing up—everything around me sounded muffled.

I was terrified, imagining what was going on. I started questioning myself again for having brought her to the United States. Yet again, I wondered if I had I made a mistake by bringing her here. How did I think I would be able to raise a child in a culture so different than my own? In a language I don't speak? With customs and rules so different from what I knew?

As I sat on the step, I knew I had to have a plan of how I would speak with Luz about the phone call. I couldn't think clearly.

The teacher had called around ten in the morning, so I had several hours before I'd get home from work and could talk to Luz about this, face-to-face. I was glad for the time, because I wasn't sure I could remain calm enough in the moment. I had heard of these things happening before with some of my coworkers' children, but I had convinced myself that Luz would never get involved in such *tonterías*.

I thought again about all of the nonsense she could have been involved in. I remember thinking that the kids who did those things must have been doing them before they came to the United States, or that their parents hadn't raised them well. I knew that Luz would never get involved in such things. After all, Luz was only twelve. She was still a little girl and didn't know about those things. Besides, I had raised her to be a serious student and to make good choices.

After I left El Salvador, I knew that my mother would have continued to guide her. They went to church regularly, and I knew that Luz knew the difference between right and wrong. But doubt slowly started creeping in. Maybe I was fooling myself. As I continued to think about it, I started to wonder if I really knew Luz at all.

As the day went on, I replayed the conversation with the teacher again and again. My emotions fluctuated between sadness, rage, confusion, and heartache. Again, I started thinking about my coworkers and their kids who were at these sex parties, and I started to wonder if maybe those "bad kids" weren't bad after all. Maybe Luz wasn't so bad, either.

Maybe they just got mixed up in things that were bigger than they were. Maybe they were reacting to not knowing their place in this strange, new country. Just like teenagers everywhere, maybe they were looking for a sense of independence and belonging, and these parties were filling a gap. Perhaps they were questioning their parents and reacting to the sense of self-doubt that creeps in when you come to a new country and, in so many cases, a new family.

I started questioning myself and realizing that, while I made the best decision I could have, given my circumstances, maybe I had really hurt Luz by leaving her. But even so, why couldn't she see what she was doing by skipping school and getting mixed up in such dangerous things? Why would she let the opportunity of being in *los Estados Unidos* go to waste?

I was ready to talk to Luz. I had to stop her from taking this slippery path. She needed to understand that she was one of the lucky kids, free from the violence of our country. As I thought about this conversation, my hope was that maybe, just maybe, she had a reasonable explanation. Perhaps she wasn't even running around, getting into *travesura,* mischief, but instead had a good reason for not being in school. I couldn't come up with one possibility. But I held out hope that maybe Luz had a reason. She must have had a reason.

Seventeen

Luz

When my mother confronted me about my absences from school, I had just survived my first winter in *el Norte*. I had never experienced anything like the bitter Mid-Atlantic winter. When I arrived, in October, the weather was mild—cooler than I was used to, but not frigid. Then, as the months went on, I was shocked by how varied the temperature could be, even within the same week.

As winter took hold, the icy wind whipped around me as I waited for the school bus. I remember thinking that the temperature had dropped as much as it possibly could. Then, without fail, the next day's temperature would be even lower.

On top of the freezing cold, the snow fell—many, many inches of it. Having watched American movies when I was younger, I had been so excited to see snow for real, for the first time. I imagined the serenity of a white blanket, covering and protecting everything beneath it. I was sure that something so peaceful and lovely had to be a safe haven. But the beauty of the snow belied its oppressive nature; while it covered everything, rather than protecting, it seemed to suffocate.

Everything was more difficult in the snow. Walking to the bus stop left my feet cold and wet. Whenever I took my gloves off, my fingers turned numb. Driving on snow-covered-roads proved dangerous, and often we were stranded at home until the temperature rose and the roads thawed out. As the snow melted, it left a dirty, tarnished outline of everything it touched.

As the temperature dropped and the snow erased the neighborhood under its white blanket, I wondered why people chose to live in such an inhospitable climate. Had the earliest inhabitants been tricked, as I had been, by the more temperate autumn? Even worse than the freezing temperatures and the wet, icy snow, the sky simultaneously seemed to close up as the days got shorter and shorter. In the mornings, I would wake in the frigid darkness, and only minutes after arriving home from school, it became dark again. How could anyone live like this?

Now, in March, spring started bringing glimmers of hope with ever-so-slightly warmer days. But just when I started thinking that things could be bearable, my mother started questioning me about my whereabouts.

Mami had come home early that day and prepared a lovely dinner for me. When I arrived home from school, she had my favorite meal on the table for me: *pupusas*, salad, rice, and beans. As I walked through the door, the savory aroma greeted me, as did the humidity of the apartment—I had recently noticed that, when the temperature outside dropped and whenever anyone cooked in the apartment, the air thickened. Humidity condensed on the sliding glass door, obscuring our view to the street below.

The delicious smells reminded me of my *abuelita* and her wonderful home-cooked meals. Every meal she made was prepared with love, and the smell of the *pupusas* wrapped around me like my *abuelita's* arms embracing me. I was starting to realize how strongly memories are linked to smells, and how food could be such a comfort. They were links to my past and quickly evoked feelings of joy. For a brief instant, I felt that I was home again, that *abuelita* was waiting for me.

I was excited to inspect the steaming pots and pans to see for myself what flavors were to come. I slid next to my *mami*, who was at the stove, stirring the rice. I nudged closer to her than I normally would have; anticipating the meal made me feel closer to her. My mother was not as good a cook as my *abuelita,* but I was becoming accustomed to her way of preparing food and knew that I would enjoy this meal.

But it seemed that my mother had planned an ambush with her delicious meal. As I sat down at the table, my mother passed me my plate and said, very quietly, "Your teacher called today."

I hesitated.

"*¿Sí?*" I asked.

"Yes, "she answered. "She said that you've been very withdrawn."

I lowered my head, looking at the plate in front of me, pushing the rice around with a fork. My mother continued.

"She also said that you've been missing school." My mother chuckled nervously. Her voice was shaking, but she continued, telling me what the teacher had said.

It was a cruel joke, having my *abuelita's* food in front of me, but now my desire to consume it had vanished in light of this confrontation. My mother continued talking, and all I could do was stare at the plate.

She wanted to know where I had been when I wasn't in school. She asked about the parties and the kids in the neighborhood and the drinking and the marijuana. I looked at her in silence. I couldn't tell her where I had been when I wasn't in school. I hadn't been at the parties, or drinking, or doing drugs, or smoking cigarettes.

I could not believe that she would think I was capable of doing such things. How could she not think better of me than that? It hurt me that my mother thought I was capable of doing things that I *knew* were wrong. Why would she think that about me?

As she continued speaking, her volume increased slightly with each sentence. She started rattling dishes around and then got up, clanging around the kitchen. She started getting upset. I just looked at her as she accused me of sleeping around and of being a *puta,* a whore.

I just watched her and stayed silent. The angrier she got, the more certain I was that I could not tell her what was happening. Silence was my only defense, as I was sure that anything I said at this point was useless. Before my eyes, my mother was turning into a monster.

Eighteen

Esperanza

I could not believe what had happened. I had started talking to Luz very calmly. Purposefully, I started my interrogation so that we could be conversing about where she was. I hadn't wanted to accuse her of anything before I gave her a chance to explain. But quickly, things changed and went in a direction I hadn't expected.

When I asked her where she had been, she just looked down at the plate I had given her. As I continued talking, she closed further and further in on herself, just staring at the food in front of her. She didn't respond to anything I said. Her eyes glazed over.

Not only wouldn't she tell me where she had been when she wasn't in school, but also she didn't say a word. The less responsive she became, the more enraged I felt. I started imagining what she had been doing when she wasn't in school—with boys in some dirty apartment, drinking and getting so drunk that she passed out. The thought of these things made me ill.

All she did was look at me blankly. It was as if she wasn't there. Her body was there and her eyes were transfixed on one grain of rice, but Luz disappeared.

I couldn't handle her silence any more. Her unresponsiveness convinced me that she was getting into serious trouble. So I tried to get her to communicate with me. I hit the table in front of her with the wooden cooking spoon to see if the noise would bring her back to reality. She flinched slightly but continued her hollow stare.

Failing to pull her attention back, I suddenly, unexpectedly took the spoon and hit her on top of her head. I have no idea why I did that. I don't know what possessed me, in that moment. She cowered. Then I struck her with the spoon, again and again. I called her awful names. I told her that she was a whore and deserved to be hit. I screamed and yelled, and said that maybe she wouldn't skip school if she got a good beating.

As my blows came down on her head, she finally started moving. She covered her head with her hands and I continued striking her, on her neck and her back, and on her hands. The more submissive she was, the more aggressive I became. Her meekness fueled my rage.

Suddenly, I stopped. I don't know how long I had been hitting her, but at some point, I looked at Luz and then at the wooden spoon in my hand.

Oh my God! What was I doing? What had happened to me? I had *never* hit Luz. Never. I had never hit anyone or anything. What was happening to me?

Who was I becoming? I love Luz more than anyone in the world, and I had just beaten her with a wooden spoon. I looked at her again and saw welts starting to form on her neck. Her hands were bloodied from where I had broken the skin as she covered her head. I looked at my hands and dropped the spoon to the ground. I fell to the ground next to her. I started crying and asking myself aloud what had happened. Luz remained huddled in the chair, covering her head.

I had crossed a line. What was happening to us? Our family was falling apart. Just as I was getting our family back together, I was breaking it apart. I had brought Luz here to escape violence, but look what I was becoming—I was becoming the very thing I had tried to avoid.

This country was changing me.

Nineteen

Luz

Somehow I was able to get myself to the bathroom at the end of the hall. My head was pounding and my hands had gone numb.

Never had I imagined that my mother would ever strike me. I couldn't remember her hitting me before. Except for that night in the desert, I couldn't remember ever being hit before by *anyone*.

I tried to think, to figure out why she had hit me. What happened? I couldn't make sense of anything. I saw lights flashing in front of me. I steadied myself against the sink and tried to look in the mirror to see what my mother had done.

I couldn't focus my eyes. Lights continued flashing, and as I tried to fix my gaze on the mirror, I couldn't bring my image into focus. Silence filled the air as my ears started closing up. I felt like I was underwater. I turned on the faucet, thinking I would splash water on my face. As I released one hand from the sink, everything went black.

* * * *

I woke up in the bed that I shared with my mother. I don't know how I got there or how long I had been there. As I opened my eyes, I could see my mother, pacing in the corner. She looked worried. She had her hand across her mouth, and she had clearly been crying. When she turned and saw that I had awoken, she ran to my side and burst into tears.

I heard her say that she was sorry and that she loved me as she grabbed my arm and pulled me up. Wrapping her arm around my neck and bringing me close to her, she rocked me. She continued crying—wailing—apologizing again and again. She said she didn't know what had happened. And I sat, paralyzed, next to her with her arm around my neck.

After a minute, her crying changed and her nose started to clog up, so she could only breathe through her mouth. She was so upset. She started to cough. Quickly turning and sitting up, on the side of the bed, she put her feet on the ground as her coughing intensified. Then she started retching, as if she was going to vomit. For a moment, she sat at the edge of the bed coughing with intermittent moments of deep breathing.

Gradually, her breathing became more regular and the heaving and coughing subsided. She slowly turned around and looked at me, and I could see her swollen, bloodshot eyes. Looking at me, she took my hand in hers.

"Luz, I am so sorry for what I did to you," she said. "I never, ever thought that I would hit you like that. I don't know what happened to me."

I didn't know what to do, so I brought myself up, sat on the edge of the bed, beside her, and lowered my head. I realized that no one could keep me safe. I had been vulnerable in the desert when the *coyote* raped me, and I was defenseless now, sitting with my mother.

I had prayed that my *papi* was somehow looking over me from heaven. But again, he had failed to keep me safe. I had wondered if he was looking over me in the desert. Now I was certain that he wasn't.

Sitting with *mami,* I desperately wanted to be held, but at the same time, I wanted to push her away. I yearned for her comfort—I wanted to know that she would protect me. But I also knew that she was the one from whom I needed protection.

Twenty

Esperanza

I barely slept that night. Every time I closed my eyes and started drifting into sleep, images of Luz cowering on the kitchen floor came flooding back and I jolted awake. Each time this happened, I reached over and felt for Luz next to me, her soft breathing, rhythmic, as sleep enveloped her.

Around four in the morning, after many false starts, I was awakened again by the horror of what I had just done. Sitting up in bed, I put my hand on Luz's smooth, dark hair. Diego's moonbeam, as I came to call it, shone in and cast a ray of blue light across her body. As she lay there, her delicate face looked so peaceful, disguising the anguish that must have been lying beneath the surface.

In sleep, with her hands curled up beneath her chin, she looked so much younger, like the Luz of the *campo*. I asked God to protect her from me and wondered if Luz would ever be able to forgive me for what I had done. I was so lucky to have her with me. It was my role to protect her, to keep her safe, yet again I had broken her trust, and this time unforgivably.

I thought about all of the other Salvadoran and Central American mothers who weren't with their children—those who had left their babies in the *campos*, praying for their safety as someone else raised them. I knew how it felt to put faith in the hope that someone else would treat your child the way that you would, wondering if their decisions, even the small ones along the way, would be the same ones you would make.

I thought of the mothers who brought their children with them as they attempted to cross the border together, and of those whose children had succumbed to the dangers along the way. I prayed for those whose children were cruelly taken away from them, so close to freedom, as they were arrested for merely seeking asylum—safety, away from the dangers of their *campos*.

I thought about the husbands and wives, separated from one another as they tried to build their lives across continents, and of the brothers and sisters who bravely crossed the border together, each others' protectors, only to be forcibly separated once they arrived in *el Norte*, taken from the only other person they knew.

My heart ached, thinking of these people, good people who so desperately wanted to be together and couldn't be. I could never take for granted that Luz was with me. How could I have hurt her? I had to do better. I *have* to do better.

Twenty-One

Luz

As I rolled over in bed, I was woken by a searing pain shooting from the center of my upper back into the base of my head. Surprised by such an awful sensation, I squeezed my eyes shut, attempting to ease the stabbing feeling. But another jolt pierced deep into my head, landing just behind my right eye.

Slowly opening my eyes, I looked across the room and saw a neatly folded pile of freshly washed clothes on the chair near our bedroom window. I turned my head slightly to see if I could see *mami* in the room, but the searing pain stopped me cold. I rubbed the base of my neck to ease the throbbing and remembered the *golpes*, the blows, my mother had given me. It took me a moment to recall what had fueled her rage, and then I remembered that she had been asking me about missing school.

I started to rock back and forth, hoping to soothe the throbbing in my neck and head. It helped a little. My mother's blows had been intense, and their aftereffects would not be going away soon.

My mother's hand was on my head. She was stroking my hair, wanting to right the awful wrong she had committed. When I realized that she was touching me, I quickly pulled away and curled into a ball, my back to her. Even through the pain, I knew that I didn't want her touching me. How dare she try to make me feel better when she was responsible for my pain? Wrapping my hands around my head, I applied pressure in an effort to ease the throbbing.

As I continued rocking I thought of my *abuelita*, wondering how my life had changed so tragically in such a short amount of time. Would things ever get better?

Twenty-Two

Esperanza

After Luz fell back to sleep, my mind drifted back to those who had attempted to cross the border to *el Norte*. I remembered Dolores, one of the mothers who had traveled with me. On this dark morning, her story was even more painful than ever to recall.

* * * *

We had been traveling for days by foot across the desert. Dolores had traveled these many miles with her son, Jesús, a sweet little boy of about seven or eight. He had been playful from the start of our journey, and where any other child would have complained, he continued on steadfastly as we faced more and more challenging conditions.

Jesús seemed almost oblivious to the dangers and difficulties in our path, encouraging his mother through the toughest parts. Clearly, he was why she was risking their lives to go to *el Norte*. He understood her sacrifice and did everything he could to make things easier for his *mamá*.

We were joined by another caravan of immigrants and then herded to a large freezer truck. The bright colors decorating the trailer's outside walls are seared in my

111

memory. Fruit and vegetables were painted on the sides—a visual explosion of colors, along with big white letters. I couldn't understand the words spelled by the letters, but I guessed that they referenced a large grocery store.

I'll never forget Jesús's and his mother's reactions as we approached the eighteen-wheeler. Two people couldn't have had more different responses to the same situation.

The boy was happy to finally stop walking, and his excitement was irrepressible, knowing that he would get into the cargo area of the truck. His mother, however, was gravely concerned about boarding the big rig. She tried to temper her son's excitement, but he couldn't contain himself.

I imagined that Jesús was one of those little boys who would stare in wonder when work trucks came through to repair roads in the *campo*. He would probably run wild, gathering his friends to go and watch the heavy machinery at work. I never really understood what inspired such wonder in those little boys as they watched the labors progress, hour after hour. The only thing Jesús was missing that day was his group of friends to marvel at this wondrous machine.

Today, this brilliantly colored cargo truck captivated him. He barraged his mother with questions: How big was the truck? Would they ride in it? How many people would be in the truck? Did it have lights? Did it run on gasoline or diesel? Could he sit with the driver? What about the horn? How many tires did it have? Why were the tires doubled up? For every answer provided, the boy asked at least five more questions of greater complexity. I watched the exchange for several minutes as I and the other adults waited impatiently to board the trailer.

Watching them, I wondered if I should have brought Luz with me on this journey. It had initially surprised me to see Jesús traveling to *el Norte*, but as he was weathering the trip so well, I thought perhaps I had made a mistake, not bringing her.

As we milled around outside of the trailer, I took in the beauty of the foreign landscape around me. I wondered if I was on another planet, as the mountainous terrain differed greatly from the mountains of El Salvador. At home, the *naturaleza* is brimming with greenery and life below the surface. In this desert, the surrounding mountains were stunning in their arid, rugged beauty. The desolation of the landscape seemed to go on for interminable stretches, scorched by the relentlessly blazing sun. I stood in awe, considering how it was that I was in such a different and unknown place.

Finally, as the sky looked afire with the pinks and purples of dusk, and after hours of waiting in the unforgiving heat, we boarded the trailer. I had heard that tractor trailers were typical for this part of the journey, but had hoped to be spared what I was sure was going to be the worst part of the trip.

The temperature had dropped some as the sun set, but the breezeless, dry heat was still fierce. As I got in and moved slowly to the back, the inside air felt stifling. Further to the rear of the truck, it felt even hotter than just a few feet closer to the door. Very quickly the trailer filled up with fifty or so others in search of *el sueño Americano*.

When the truck filled beyond capacity, I felt my heart start to race. Beads of sweat forming on my lip and brow were not only from the heat, but also from the terror brimming up as the reality of confinement set in. So many of us were in the trailer that everyone was touching another, close in, like cattle in an overloaded pen.

Jesús and his mother were sitting across from me. Even in the trailer's dim light, I saw the fear in his mother's eyes as the space around her and Jesús filled up. But Jesús, oblivious to what was happening, was still excited to be in the truck.

Suddenly, the trailer door closed and everything went black. I heard the latch slam down, sealing the truck, sealing our fate. The truck began to move—speeding down the lonely road, somewhere, in the dark of night. A constant rumbling. I breathed deeply—the alternative was to panic, and I knew that panicking would only make things worse. I began to whisper the "Hail Mary."

"Dios te salve, María, llena eres de gracia, el Señor es contigo. Bendita tú eres entre todas las mujeres, y bendito es el fruto de tu vientre, Jesús. Santa Maria, Madre de Dios, ruega por nosotros, pecadores, ahora y en la hora de nuestra muerte. Amen."

I repeated the prayer over and over, asking María to protect us on our journey. The temperature inside the truck quickly rose as the multitude of bodies in the enclosed space began generating heat.

I heard Jesús's voice change from excitement to terror. His voice wavered, his questions changing soon after the latch closed down: *Mami,* why did they lock us in? *Mami,* what if I have to pee? *Mami,* will we be able to get out? *Mami,* it's so dark. *Mami, mami, mami . . . auxilio!* Help!

His mother's responses were few and far between. She whispered in his ear, and all I could hear was inaudible shushing. Then I heard her start to whimper. When she started crying, Jesús stopped asking questions, reverting back to her protector.

"*Mamá*, it'll be okay. Don't worry, *mamá*. No, *mamá*, be strong."

As Jesús was comforting his mother, I realized that he was also comforting me and others around us. I will never understand how such a young child kept so many adults calm.

Twenty-Three

Luz

Unable to face my mother, crying behind me, all I could do was stare through our bedroom window. The moon's light seemed to magnify in intensity as it passed through the cloudy, somewhat opaque glass. It illuminated our otherwise dark space with a surprising brightness.

As I examined the moon's mottled, cratered surface, I remembered how it looked, that terrible night in the desert. Its light reflected off of the rocks and shrubs and hid the *coyote's* face until he turned. Then it revealed his identity. Obscuring and then clarifying.

Tonight, it was once again a silent observer of my mistreatment, the only witness to my mother's brutality. The only witness, but unable to speak. Just like me—unable to reveal what had happened. Unable to admit that, maybe, somehow, I was responsible for everything that was happening to me.

I wondered what other atrocities the moon had illuminated, over the eons. What other misfortunes had it silently revealed and then hid away, secreted forever? It must be quite a burden to bear, being the sole witness to the worst of humanity and then forced to keep it a secret, its illuminating light forever obscuring the awful realities unfolding below.

And as I lay in bed, watching its rays shine through our bedroom, I prayed for the moon to take this new horror and hide it away with the others it had once exposed and then kept secret.

Twenty-Four

Esperanza

Time passed in an immeasurable way as we sat in the hot trailer. Each minute seemed like an hour and each hour seemed like a day. The temperature rose, the air continued to thicken, and what started as a small sense of panic started filling the trailer. I was shocked when the men started panicking first. I had been raised to think that men were stronger and less emotional than women.

When the air in the trailer seemed to nearly evaporate, the men began shouting. Soon their shouts became cries, pleas for someone's, anyone's attention. Jesús and his mother continued whispering in each other's ears. I couldn't see anything, but the hysteria within the trailer intensified—screaming and yelling filling the void left by the disappearing air.

I sporadically continued reciting the "Hail Mary" quietly to calm myself down. At some point, I felt the man who was sitting next to me shift position. The sweat from our touching arms had long ago commingled. I heard him whisper something to me.

"*Que?*" I asked.

He continued whispering, but I still couldn't understand him.

"*¿Estás bien?*" I asked.

His whispering continued, and all I could make out was a rhythmic *shushshushshush*. After a few minutes, I realized that he, too, was whispering the "Hail Mary." I started praying again, trying to match his rhythm and cadence.

After a few repetitions, I heard others joining us. The rhythm of the prayer seemed to bring comfort in this hopeless situation. I tried to imagine the factors that had brought each of us to the truck that day. I wondered if anything was so bad that it would have made this misery worth enduring. Was whatever we were fleeing worth this certain death that was now upon us?

Our prayers continued. At one point, our voices were strong and hopeful, but soon after, the stifling conditions started quieting us, one by one, as we begged for respite from this nightmare. Beleaguered and hopeless, our hoarse voices began to fade as we implored the Virgin for her protection. I was certain that, for some, it was their last moments.

I did my best to continue praying, especially for those who could no longer pray for themselves. With each silenced voice, I envisioned a person who had inhaled for the last time in this vacuum poisoning us with our own breaths. At first, the thought terrified me, but soon it brought me calm, knowing that those defenseless souls had finally found peace.

When I could only muster strength to say four or five words of the prayer, I felt my time was approaching. I was moving in and out of consciousness, and each time I came to, I did my best to continue praying. After a while, when I awoke, I didn't hear anyone praying, and wondered how many of us were alive.

Then I remembered Jesús and his mother. Listening for their quiet whispers, I heard nothing.

"Jesús?" I asked. No response.

"Jesús?" I tried saying louder. I drifted out of consciousness and then back again, into my horrific reality.

"Jesús?" I again asked, reaching in front of me, where I knew he and his mother had been. I felt Dolores' foot in front of me in the dark and shook her leg.

"*¿Dolores? ¿Que ha pasado con Jesús?*" What's going on with Jesús?

She didn't respond.

"*¿Dolores?*" I beseeched. "*¿Que ha pasado con Jesús?*"

"*Está con el Señor*," she quietly whispered back. He's with the Lord.

In that moment, I knew that this journey was not worth it. Jesús had just given his life for *el sueño Americano*—his dream for his future had killed him.

As Dolores wept, I squeezed her foot.

"*Dolores, lo siento, Dolores.*" I said, holding her foot tightly, attempting to connect with her. I'm so sorry.

Finally, the truck slowed and I felt the squeal of the brakes as they impeded the enormous weight, the inertia, of the truck moving forward. Gravel crunched beneath the tires as they slowed to a halt. Within the trailer, tensions rose with a stirring of anticipation for something to happen, for the door to open. Seconds turned into minutes, but there was nothing. Certainly, we were not being left here to die in back of this truck.

I imagined the driver realizing what had happened and, in desperation, leaving us on the side of the road while he sought protection for himself for what had happened. As each second passed, I envisioned the precious remaining air in the truck slowly disappearing. Again, panic rose within me.

Finally, the latch turned. The door cracked open, at first very slowly, and then with a sudden burst, it swung wildly as those inside the trailer pushed it with every ounce of force they could muster. Flashlights beamed in, announcing the conclusion of this horrendous ride.

Looking at the door, I gathered all of my remaining strength to get up onto my knees. I was so weak that I could not stand. I pushed myself toward the light, which was blinding, not knowing what lay ahead. As the fresh air reached me, I took a deep breath. The outside heat felt like frigid compared to the inferno within. I fell forward, then stumbled out of the truck.

Some of my traveling companions came off the truck with me, but many did not. Men in uniforms were attempting to corral us together. I couldn't imagine what would happen next, but it would be far better than what would have happened if we stayed in the trailer.

As my foot touched the ground, the residual heat of the day, trapped in the asphalt even in the darkness of night, penetrated through my shoes. I tried to orient myself and looked around for some clues as to where I was. In the darkness of night, I could only see the rays of light coming from the flashlights of the uniformed officers.

As the others exited the truck, one of the uniformed men called to his colleague as he inspected the trailer. I looked back into the truck and saw countless bodies lying lifeless on the floor.

When I looked where I had been inside, I saw Dolores sitting on the floor, her back leaning against the wall. On her lap was little Jesús. They were chest to chest, their arms wrapped around one another's necks. The boy's legs straddled his mother and his feet were pushed up against the trailer wall on either side of her back. His head was perched between his own arm and his mother's face. Mother and son were wet with perspiration, and their dark hair glistened in the flashlight's light.

I then realized that Jesús was quite a big boy. Intertwined with his mother, he looked long and lanky, on the cusp of pre-adolescence. They didn't move to get off of the truck. They sat there silently, most certainly in death, a fate that had befallen so many, that awful night.

As noise and commotion surrounded me, I continued looking at Dolores and Jesús, wondering if I could have helped them. Their quiet whispers during the ride had calmed me, yet I had done nothing to ease their suffering. I wondered why I survived and they hadn't.

I continued staring at them while people talked and yelled around me, and then I saw Dolores move her foot. She shook her head and called for help; she had survived.

* * * *

I looked down at my sleeping daughter, safe in our apartment but black and blue from my brutality. I had saved her from a fate that Jesús was unable to escape, and she had survived her own journey—enduring something terrible, of which she had yet to speak—and I had inflicted more violence upon her. How could I have done this to her, especially since Jesús had been sacrificed, like so many others, in hopes of something better? I must find redemption.

Twenty-Five

Luz

The next day, I went to school. My mother told me that I should stay home and heal. I told her I would, but after she left for work, I got on the bus anyway. The throbbing in my head had subsided, and I realized that if I stayed home I wouldn't have anything to do. Even though I hated school, at least I wouldn't be alone.

I had spent days home, before. Those were the days that my mother had asked me about. When I wasn't in school, I was home—I had stayed home because the thought of facing the students and teachers at school was just too much.

Before arriving in the United States, I envisioned going to school in *el Norte* and making friends right away. I never had trouble making friends in *el campo*, and my mother told me that there were a lot of kids at the school who spoke Spanish and I would find a best friend right away. When I first met Marisol, I thought maybe *mami* was right. But I was soon disappointed when Marisol and I didn't have any classes together.

Other Spanish-speaking students seemed to shy away from me. I felt as if I wore some sort of repellant that made me unpalatable to them. The white kids at school mostly ignored me. Sometimes it felt like they were looking past me, as if I didn't exist. When they acknowledged me, I felt their resentment for my being in "their" school.

The black kids, very much like the white kids, tended to ignore me as well. Sometimes there were some, both white and black, who seemed enraged that I and other immigrant students didn't speak English. They taunted us in the hallways, calling us names, telling us to speak English and that we should go back to Mexico. Some of them would come up close to me and start speaking gibberish, pretending it was Spanish. Unable to defend myself in English, all I could do was walk away. I felt powerless.

I had been sure that the teachers would be nice—I don't know why I thought that, as the teachers in El Salvador had never been particularly nice to students who were different. I guess I just never noticed. In *el campo*, I wasn't one of the different kids. Looking back, I realized that students who struggled in school or who were poorer than the rest tended to annoy the teachers. Here, it was the same, only now I was one of the different kids.

The teachers seemed bothered by me. Many of them treated me as if I were stupid because I didn't speak English, losing patience with me and my classmates who were also learning English. They seemed to feel that Spanish was an inferior language and those who spoke it lacked intelligence.

Even when I didn't understand their words, I had no trouble understanding what they meant when they sighed at me or smacked their lips when I asked for help. I saw their sidelong glances at me when they spoke with other teachers. I couldn't understand why I seemed to rouse such dislike. Was it me personally? Or did I represent something to them, something that I wasn't aware of?

Going to school was painful because, no matter what, no matter how much I tried to be friendly, I was despised. But the day after my mother beat me, I felt that school was the only place I could be.

That day, as I walked through the school's halls, surrounded by hundreds of other students, I felt lonelier than ever. As I walked by the metal lockers lining the hall, running my hands along the dangling locks, I wondered if I could crawl inside one of them and hide there.

The bruises and welts on my head and neck were very tender. My hands had small cuts, and my knuckles were purple from where I had tried to protect myself from the ever-pounding wooden spoon.

When I got to my first class, no one seemed to notice my bruises. My teacher greeted me at the door, as she did every day that I came to school, and I proceeded to my assigned seat. The students sitting on either side of me also seemed oblivious. I don't know what I had expected, no one had ever noticed me before and I don't know why I thought today would be any different.

Though I tried to focus on the teacher's lesson and classwork, my mind kept returning to my mother's outburst. I still couldn't fathom what had made her so angry and why she got angrier and angrier with each blow she gave me.

Walking along the hall's perimeter, trying to avoid the typical chaos of the halls between classes, I saw my math teacher as I approached my third-period class. He stopped me at the door before I walked in. Always checking in with students as they entered the classroom, he asked me how I was. Today his inquiry seemed different—he seemed to actually be concerned for me.

I assured him that I was fine, at least I tried to. My English was not very good, but I thought I made it clear to him that I was okay. As he continued questioning me, I tried to hide my growing anxiety, and hoped that I convinced him that nothing was wrong. He started the class and, as was my habit, I blended into the background.

After a break for lunch, I returned from the cafeteria to my math class. A few minutes after the late bell sounded, a call came over the loudspeaker, and I was asked to go to the nurse's office. I had seen other students get called from class like this and wondered where they might be going. Today my concern was, "What is the nurse's office?" I looked at the teacher and gave my very best look of confusion. Understanding, he asked another student to walk me there.

The nurse was a plump, blonde woman with a great big smile. Since I had arrived in the United States and at this school, no one had been quite as happy to see me as she was, that afternoon.

She spoke to me in English. I struggled to answer her questions, but could only understand every fifth or sixth word. I knew that she was asking how I was. She motioned to my back and my neck, and I presumed that she wanted to see my injuries. I wrapped my jacket tightly around me to keep her away from my black-and-blue neck.

She put her arm around me and gave me a sideways hug. I could tell that she was doing her best to make me feel safe and comfortable, but I couldn't trust a stranger who couldn't understand me and who I couldn't understand.

Squeezing me again, she left me in the back room of her office. It looked like a doctor's office, with an examining table and counter space with medical equipment. I waited, sitting on the table, holding my jacket around me, and squeezing my arms tightly across my chest.

After a while, a small woman with dark hair and glasses came in. She was probably forty or fifty years old and smelled of coffee. Pulling up a chair in front of me, she looked me squarely in the eyes and spoke to me in Spanish. She asked how I was doing. She said that she had heard that I had bruises on my neck and asked if she could see them.

I tried to tell her that there was nothing there, but she persisted. She said that I could trust her and if someone was hurting me, then she and the nurse would do everything they could to protect me. I continued to deny that I had bruises and told her that no one had hurt me. While I said that, I felt tears rolling down my cheeks.

I stood, and as I tried to leave, I stumbled as I tried to maneuver around her. She braced me as I fell into her. Holding me up, she looked at me again. My cheeks were wet and my eyes stung. She hugged me gently and told me that it would be okay. I sobbed into her shoulder, and she held onto me as I cried.

When I calmed down some, she sat me back down and asked if she could see the bruises. I pulled the collar of my shirt back and lifted my hair so she could see my neck. I continued crying softly as she called the nurse back in. The nurse examined my neck, looked at the cuts on my hands, and carefully pulled my hair to the side, where she discovered a small gash that opened up from one of my mother's blows.

The nurse looked at me and asked what had happened. The small dark-haired woman interpreted for me. I looked back at them both but refused to answer. They rephrased the question, but I stayed silent. Then they asked if I felt safe at home. How could I say that I didn't feel safe at home? What would they do? I told them that I did.

Twenty-Six

Esperanza

The phone call came in at about two in the afternoon. Someone from the school spoke to me in Spanish and told me they were calling on behalf of the nurse. They said that Luz had been taken to the hospital and that it appeared that she had been attacked.

My heart jumped into my throat. Attacked? I asked what they meant by attacked. They said that she had bruises on her neck and head, and it seemed that someone had hit her from behind. They explained that she was hesitant to say what had happened, but they had concluded that there was an incident in one of the bathrooms at school. They assured me that they were investigating what had happened, but that right now, it was critical that I meet them and Luz at the hospital.

Suddenly the gravity of what I had done came to me. I had told Luz to stay home—I didn't realize that she had gone to school. Maybe going to school had saved her life. Maybe something had happened as a result of my hitting her, and because she was at school, someone was able to help her. What had I done?

I explained to the school caller that I would do my best to get there as fast as I could, but without a car, it would take a little while. Then I asked my supervisor for permission to leave and asked a friend from the neighborhood, Julio, to pick me up from work and take me to the hospital. I was so thankful that it was raining that day, which meant Julio wasn't working and could get me there quickly.

When we arrived, Julio asked if I'd like him to come in with me. I hadn't even thought about it, but when he offered, I agreed that it would be nice to have him there with me.

Somehow, we managed to navigate our way through the maze of halls at the hospital to the emergency room and found Luz. Julio stayed back as I pulled the curtain in the small room where Luz was lying in bed. A few other people were in the room, but when I saw Luz, her brown skin against the white sheets, I didn't care who else was there. I ran to her and put my arms around her. She flinched and became rigid as our cheeks touched. I wondered if those at her bedside noticed her change in demeanor.

I backed away a little, grabbing her by the upper arms, and looked at her. She looked back at me, but her eyes really looked through me. This blank look—the one where she wasn't really seeing what was in front her—was becoming common for Luz, and while it no longer surprised me, I was in tears.

"Buenas tardes," a raspy voice said quietly from behind.

Still holding on to Luz, I looked over my shoulder, turning toward the voice, and saw a plump woman with greying dark hair and glasses sitting next to Luz's bed. She looked vaguely familiar, but I couldn't quite place her. My eyes moved to the person in the other chair, a chubby blonde-haired woman. I slowly let go of Luz and turned toward the women. The dark-haired one spoke again, and I realized that they both worked at the school. When I had enrolled Luz, the dark-haired one had explained things to Luz and me in Spanish.

The women said that one of Luz's teachers had noticed that she was acting differently in class. She had always been quiet, but today she was more timid and reserved than usual, almost frightened. The teacher had noticed the bruises on Luz's hands and neck. Because of this, they explained, the school was obligated to take action.

Over the next several hours, doctors and nurses checked in on Luz. They examined her bruises, shined lights in her eyes, took blood from her, and stitched up the cut that I had caused. At some point, I was pulled out of Luz's room and was questioned by a police officer and by someone I think may have been a social worker.

They asked me questions about Luz. When did she arrive in the United States? How long had we been apart? Who were her friends? Had she been acting strangely before today? Did I suspect that people she was involved with were dangerous or in gangs? Did I know who would want to hurt Luz? Had I heard about the teenagers who had been missing in the area? Was Luz a friend of theirs?

I tried to answer their questions the best that I could. I hadn't stopped crying since I first saw Luz, looking like a shell of her former self, staring blankly at me from her hospital bed. Each question seemed to feed my tears.

They did not seem to know that I was responsible for her injuries. Luz had not told them. Why had she protected me? We both knew that I would deserve any punishment that would come. I also knew that this might mean that Luz could be taken from me. Did she know that, too? I had done something so terrible to my daughter that she could be taken from me.

When they were done with their questions, I was allowed to go back into Luz's room. When I entered, she looked at me with a look of terror in her eyes. All of the color had left her face, and she suddenly seemed to be very, very scared. I asked her what had happened. She looked at me, and for a brief moment, she seemed to register that I was there. Then she looked beyond me, with her now-familiar distant stare.

"*¿Luz, que pasó?*" I asked.

She looked through me.

Twenty-Seven

Luz

In the emergency room, the doctors examined every square inch of me. They found the bite-shaped scar on my shoulder from my journey to *el Norte*. They measured the wounds on my head, neck, and hands and photographed all of the bruises. They examined each and every part of my body. And with each examination, measurement, photograph, they wrote down what they saw.

Each and every violation I had withstood was now catalogued in my medical records. I wanted to disappear, to escape, but I no longer had the strength or will to stop them from examining me. I almost felt like my body didn't even belong to me.

The examination continued for a long time. Near its end, a soft-spoken woman came in with an interpreter. I wasn't sure if she was a doctor, or a nurse, or a counselor. She smiled sweetly at me and squeezed my hand as she introduced herself, with the interpreter's help. She brought with her an energy that lightened the feeling in the room. She seemed to genuinely care about me, and I felt that if I told her what happened, she wouldn't judge me for what I had done.

She asked how I was and if I wanted to tell her what had happened. There was something about her that made me want to open up to her, and every fiber of my being wanted to scream out my story. I could feel my hands and feet starting to go numb from the nervousness of just thinking about being that vulnerable. She looked at me, waiting for my response.

I felt my stomach sinking. I was so close to talking. If she had waited another minute, or maybe just a few more seconds—given me just an instant more—I would have told her about the hurt of being abandoned, about how much I loved my *abuelita* and the gut-wrenching misery of knowing that I couldn't be with her. I would have told her about the *coyote* who took away my innocence in the desert, and the way my mother beat me because I was incapable of communicating with her. I would have told her about the shame of knowing that I was somehow responsible for all of the things that happened. I would have told her everything.

Instead, just as I was about to speak, she started talking, and I felt myself closing up. My nervousness disappeared, and the fog that was becoming an ever-present feeling enveloped me once again. I felt like a daylily that had briefly opened up with a ray of sun and then closed again as the night began to fall.

The sweet-faced doctor, nurse, counselor, or whatever she was would say a few sentences and then the interpreter would repeat what she said in Spanish. Sometimes the English and Spanish clumsily overlapped, but mostly, one would finish and the next would start.

They talked at me for a few minutes, but I wasn't sure what they said. Instead of listening to the Spanish, I kept listening for words in English and then seeing if they were what I thought they were in Spanish. They didn't seem to notice that I wasn't really paying attention to them.

As they spoke, I kept looking at the doctor-nurse-counselor and wondered why I couldn't speak to her. She kept talking to me, and she seemed to truly care about what had happened, but I couldn't manage to tell her anything. Ever since I had arrived in *los Estados Unidos*, I felt like I couldn't speak to anyone, even to those I should have been able to.

After a few minutes of the two of them going back and forth, I heard a word that stood out: *embarazada*— pregnant. When that word came out of the interpreter's mouth, I jerked my head up to look at her. She kept talking as if nothing was different. I couldn't understand what she was saying. I understood each word she said, but couldn't make sense of them all together. Had she just said that I was pregnant? My heart started pounding heavily again and my fingers and toes began to tingle.

Suddenly I felt nauseous. Just then, my mother walked back in the room. She looked at me, questioningly, through bloodshot eyes.

Twenty-Eight

Esperanza

As I stood, looking at Luz in the hospital bed, machines blinking and beeping beside her, doctors milling around her, I wondered how we had gotten to this place. How had things gone so terribly wrong so quickly?

The doctor saw me at the entrance of Luz's alcove and came over to me, gently taking my hand. She led me across the cramped space to a chair with flowered upholstery and signaled for me to sit. With the help of an interpreter, she told me that there was something I should know. She explained that Luz had given her permission to talk about this with me and that it was a very important health concern.

I was scared to hear what she was about to say. I was certain that my outburst had caused Luz some irreparable harm and was terrified to learn the extent of it. I moved to the edge of the seat, crossing my legs at the ankle, tucking them beneath the chair and grasping the armrests as I braced for the news. The interpreter said, simply, *"Luz está embarazada."*

As I heard the words leaving the interpreter's mouth, watching her lips moving as she nonchalantly told me that Luz was pregnant, my strength vanished and I slumped back in the chair. *Pregnant?*

Suddenly, the rage I had felt as Luz stared at me blankly in our kitchen the night before resurfaced. I could feel my cheeks flushing as the images I had conjured up in my mind of her with the neighborhood boys came flooding back. I had so desperately hoped that she had not been getting involved in such *travesura*, but now my doubts about her behavior were erased. My efforts to keep her safe and create a new life for her had been in vain.

My eyes moved from the interpreter to Luz. I watched her as she stared blankly ahead, seeing nothing. I wanted to grab her shoulders and shake her. I wanted to ask why she had done this. I wanted her to feel the betrayal that I was feeling.

Twenty-Nine

Luz

I returned to school about two weeks after my stay in the emergency room. After spending time in the hospital, I quickly came to hate the feeling of being back in the structured, institutional setting of my school. The dark hallways, cinder block walls, and florescent lights casting a greenish-yellow hue on everything reminded me of the sterile, uniformity of the hospital. I wasn't sure if I could bring myself to be there.

That first day back, as I moved from class to class, I wondered if anyone would even notice if I hadn't returned. None of the other kids seemed to have missed me, and the teachers missed me even less. A few asked where I had been, but no one had seemed particularly concerned that I had been away.

As the weeks went on, I sat through my classes often zoning out, distracted by my own thoughts. I still understood so little English that trying to follow what was happening in class required a herculean effort that I wasn't prepared to put forth. How could I learn pre-algebra or science when all I could think about was the baby growing inside of me?

Sometimes, before classes began, I would listen to the other girls giggle about a cute boy across the room and long for the days when my life was so simple, back in El Salvador with my *abuelita*. Everything was easier, and so much happier, then. Life was predictable, and I could always count on my *abuelita*.

Sitting in class, I would unconsciously rub my growing belly. I imagined that, when my mother was pregnant with me, she found joy in thinking about who her baby would look like, wondering if I would look more like her or my father. Perhaps she wondered if I would be a girl or a boy. She probably spent a lot of time thinking of what she would name me.

For me, though, as I rubbed my belly, I thought about how that baby got inside of me. And then I couldn't stand to think about who it would look like. What if it resembled the man who raped me? The memories of what had happened were sometimes so vivid that my chest would start to tighten as I felt the weight of that *coyote* on top of me again. Or my arms would start to burn as I remembered his knees pinning me to the ground.

The memories came back to me often, and at the most unexpected moments. And the feelings that accompanied them were so real that it felt as if he was attacking me all over again. When this happened, I couldn't listen to teachers drone on or classmates giggle. I couldn't move. I couldn't do anything.

When this happened, I felt paralyzed, trapped— knowing that this baby was now a part of me and at the same time represented the worst experience of my life. How could I love this baby? How could anyone expect me to?

At the hospital, the doctor informed my mother that I was pregnant. When she heard the word *embarazada*, she looked at me with disgust. All of her suspicions were immediately confirmed—she was certain that, when I was not in school, I had been having sex with the neighborhood boys. I saw the hurt and disappointment on her face. She'd had such high expectations and hopes for my future.

All those times she had talked to me on the phone when I was in El Salvador, she spoke of the opportunities in *el Norte*. Now my growing belly represented every missed opportunity, dashed hope, and unfulfilled dream. For her, this baby was the disappointment of unfulfilled potential.

It's unfair to bring a child into a situation like that. In the best of circumstances, raising a child is hard. But in these circumstances—conceived in violence, a teenager for a mother, a resentful, angry grandmother, a life between two cultures—what chance would this baby have?

Thirty

Esperanza

Throughout the pregnancy, I questioned Luz again and again about the identity of the baby's father. And each time, she refused to tell me. She remained silent, steadfastly refusing to disclose anything about him.

With each failed attempt to elicit a name, I would respond differently. Sometimes I would get upset and end up in one-sided arguments in which Luz would not participate. Other times, I would lose patience with her to the point that I couldn't bring myself to speak with her for days at a time. Or sometimes, feeling compassionate, I would do just hold her hand and try to understand what she might be feeling.

Occasionally, when Luz seemed ambivalent about the baby or the pregnancy, I would offer that she didn't have to have the baby if she didn't want to. I tried to tell her that she could have an abortion. But whenever I started talking about that, she'd just stare at me blankly. Those hollow stares were so difficult to glean meaning from, and I couldn't even gauge if she understood what I'd meant.

I had hoped to get my mother to discuss the option of abortion with Luz. One time, I was on the phone with

Luz's *abuela* and brought up the idea of *un aborto*. We were talking on speakerphone, and Luz was across the room, sitting on the couch.

When my mother heard the word *aborto*, she went silent, and for a few seconds I thought the call had dropped.

"Mamá," I said, checking if she was still there. When she spoke, she had sternness, almost anger, in her voice—something that I had never before heard.

"Este bebé, sin importar las circunstancias de su concepción, es una bendición. Dios quiere que nazca. ¿Quiénes somos nosotros para negar la voluntad de Dios?" This baby, regardless of the circumstances of its conception, is a blessing. It is God's will that it be born. Who are we to deny the will of God?

Hearing this, I looked over at Luz and saw her cheek twitching and her eyes widening. An unexpected rage seemed to overpower her, boiling up from somewhere deep within and bursting forth with an electric fury. She surged across the room, screaming at the phone—I had never seen her like this before.

"Is it God's will, *abuelita,* that a twelve-year-old-girl give birth?" she screamed at my mother. "Does God want children raising babies? Did God want me to be raped in the desert by that *coyote* so I could give birth to his baby? Does God will that mothers abandon their children in *el campo*? Or that fathers get murdered in broad daylight? Why, *abuela?* Why would God will such awful, terrible things? How, *abuelita,* do you know that God has willed this baby as a blessing?"

Thirty-One

Luz

I could not believe that I had spoken to my *abuelita* like that. I'd never spoken to anyone that way. My mother stood, dumbfounded, staring at me with a look of confusion that slowly softened. Her eyes welled with tears and her chin wrinkled as she seemed to hold in her emotions. She put her arms around me and pulled me close to her. She started to cry as she held me.

"Oh, Luz, I'm so, so sorry," she said when she caught her breath. "I had no idea. Please forgive me, Luz, please," she beseeched me. "This is my fault, Luz. Please, please. I'm so sorry."

She sobbed, repeating over and over how she was responsible for this happening to me. She put her hand on my belly and gently kissed it. Then she sat me down on the couch, wrapped her arms around my neck, and we sat together, crying, for a very long time. Now she knew the secret that I had been hiding. I no longer had to carry its weight by myself. I could finally give away some of the burden.

For so many months, I had convinced myself that I had somehow provoked the *coyote*. That I had done something to deserve what he did to me. Now, hearing my mother ask *me* for forgiveness, I began to realize that I wasn't at fault. She said she was responsible for what had happened.

I then realized that blaming myself for his behavior was as absurd as blaming my mother. Although we were suffering the consequences of his actions, we didn't have to take the blame for them. I couldn't hold *mami* responsible for the rape—this was not her fault. And thus, finally, I came to realize that it wasn't my fault, either.

After that, things changed between us. *Mamá* no longer looked at me with disgust or judgment, and I no longer saw those expressions of disappointment. She no longer tried to uncover the mystery of the baby's father—I think she realized that knowing the identity of the *coyote* who had raped me would not change anything.

Thirty-Two

Esperanza

In retrospect, all of the signs were there. She had that injury on her shoulder. It was the exact shape of a bite mark. She was withdrawn and upset. She cried hysterically, that first night. She was sullen and incommunicative. She was a shell of the person she had once been. Why hadn't I seen it? Or even worse, why had I chosen to ignore it?

It was so much easier to blame her—a vulnerable, naïve, twelve-year-old girl—than it was to admit that I was complicit in what I suspected had happened to her. It was easier to assume that she had been involved with the *locuras* in the neighborhood than to ask her, to *really* ask her, what had happened. I knew she had been hurt, but I was too afraid to know the extent because I was too afraid to deal with the consequences of what I had done.

In some respects, I was no better than the *coyote*.

But now I knew and had to face the reality of what happened. I couldn't change it, but I could change how I reacted to it.

I hadn't been able to protect Luz in the past—in the *campo* and on her way to *el Norte*. So I must protect her now. And I must protect her baby.

Maybe my mother was right. Maybe the baby *was* a blessing. Maybe it was my chance at redemption. Maybe with Luz's child, I could make right all that had gone wrong.

Thirty-Three

Luz

It was a humid summer day in July and just nine days after my thirteenth birthday when I went into labor. The contractions started in the early afternoon, but I didn't realize what was happening. Throughout the day, every couple of hours, a debilitating pain would seize my belly, then constrict my whole body, and then go away. My mother was working, so I walked over to our neighbor Julio's apartment. His wife was pregnant with their third child and due in the next couple of weeks.

As she opened the door, she must have seen the look on my face as a contraction took hold and asked if I was all right. I tried to nod that I was, but the pressure building in my abdomen made it difficult for me to answer. Bringing me inside of their small, cozy apartment, she led me into the kitchen and sat me down at the table. She called my mother, who asked her to call a cab to take me to the doctor's office.

Mami met me at the main entrance of the doctor's office building. Before we went inside, she called the *campo* to let my *abuelita* know that labor was starting and that her great-grandchild was on its way. Of course, we had to leave a message for *abuelita*, as she didn't have a phone in her house. We called her neighbor, who would then send one of the kids from the *campo* to my grandmother's house to let her know that we were calling. About an hour later, we would call the neighbor again and *abuelita* would be there. We were used to delayed communications, but today it was particularly frustrating, as I really wanted to talk to *abuelita* before the baby came. I knew that she would know exactly what to say to me to make me feel strong enough to give birth.

At the doctor's office, they attached machines to me to hear the baby's heartbeat and monitor the contractions. Things seemed to be progressing well and, the doctor said the contractions were far enough apart that I could go home for a bit. She said to call when they were closer together to see when I should go to the hospital.

My mother called for another taxi, and we headed back to our apartment. On our way home, she had the taxi driver stop at the grocery store. I waited in the cab as she went in. I didn't ask her what she was getting, but when she returned, I was surprised to see that she bought a beautiful *tres leches* cake. I asked what the cake was for.

"Ya viene nuestro bebé. ¡Quiero celebrar su nacimiento!" she said, excitedly. Indeed, the baby was coming, and she wanted to celebrate its birth.

Thirty-Four

Esperanza

I took Luz to the hospital in the early hours of the morning, after her contractions started coming closer together. A few hours after settling into her room, Luz delivered the most beautiful baby girl I had ever seen.

As the baby came out, I stood in awe of Luz's strength. She had already overcome so much, and watching her give birth confirmed that she was stronger than anything she had already endured. I was so proud of her.

When the doctor set the baby on top of Luz's stomach, she picked up her wrinkled infant like an experienced mother, brought her daughter's face to her own, and gave her a gentle kiss on the cheek. The baby took in her first breaths with vigorous screams and then suddenly, quietly looked at her mother.

Luz named her daughter Amparo. Protection.

Thirty-Five

Luz

From the moment I saw her, I was struck by how beautiful Amparo was, with her shock of thick, black hair. She was quite small, weighing just under six pounds, but she was very healthy and screamed almost angrily when she took her first breath. When she looked up at me for the first time, I lost myself in the depth of her dark grey eyes. She was perfect.

We stayed in the hospital for a few days as the doctors examined both of us. A social worker visited and helped *mami* and me complete forms so we could get Amparo's birth certificate and social security card. She qualified for health insurance, and the social worker gave us the name of a Spanish-speaking pediatrician for both her and me. *Mami* laughed at the thought of a little baby having so much documentation only days after being born, and thought it ironic that neither she nor I had any.

I was surprised when the nurses came in to teach me how to breastfeed Amparo. I hadn't expected that it would be difficult, as I had seen mothers in the *campo* effortlessly nurse their children. I had to learn how to hold and maneuver her so she could latch on. It was harder than I thought—an intricate dance requiring that we work together. When she was finally able to nurse, I looked down at her, taking in the enormity of this whole new tiny human being.

As Amparo nursed, I thought of baby Diego nursing in the desert, and then I thought of my father, Diego. I said my daughter's name out loud.

"Amparo."

It means protection.

I repeated her name as I looked up from her perfect face and into a mirror hanging on the wall across the room. I finally knew how my father looked at me the day we met, when I was weeks old. His expression was reflecting back at me through the mirror. I then learned what it meant to be proud of a baby who had yet to do anything, and what it meant to love someone my whole life after meeting her for only a second. I looked down at Amparo, protection, and knew that *papi* had had protected me all along. I hugged Amparo a little tighter.

A few days later, we were cleared for discharge from the hospital. I placed Amparo in the car seat that the social worker brought us, and *mami* pushed the wheelchair, taking us out of the hospital and to a waiting taxi.

Just like that—days after becoming a teenager—I was a mother, trusted to care for this tiny baby in a vast, dangerous world.

Thirty-Six

Esperanza

Despite being so young, Luz tried very hard to be a good mother to Amparo. Whenever she cried, Luz quickly went to console her. Luz changed her diapers and woke up with her in the middle of the night to nurse her. Even at such a young age, she took well to her new role. I was pleasantly surprised, and very proud of the mother she was becoming.

A few months after Amparo's birth, however, I sensed a change. I was in the kitchen, preparing dinner, and felt a strange stillness in the apartment. It was unusual that it would be so quiet. Surprised, I went back to check on Luz and Amparo.

I found Luz sitting in the wooden rocking chair that we had recently bought at a yard sale. She often sat there with Amparo to nurse her. But today, instead of tending to Amparo, she was just staring down at her. Amparo was cooing and happily smiling up at her mother.

As I followed the baby's gaze to Luz's face, I saw that Luz was crying. She was silent, but tears were falling down her cheeks. And she was trembling as she stared at Amparo.

Luz didn't notice me in the doorway. Suddenly, she started frantically inspecting Amparo's hands and then her feet. She looked at her ears, touched her nose, then lifted the happily gurgling baby from her lap and started frenetically undressing her, anxiously removing her onesie.

Holding the diapered baby in front of her, she looked at her daughter's back and traced the outline of her spine with her fingers. Then she quickly turned Amparo around and looked at the baby's chest, rubbing her hand along the small belly. As she looked at each body part, her eyes widened and she gasped, as if each time she was uncovering some hidden revelation.

As Luz became more upset, Amparo stopped smiling and cooing and started to whine, somehow aware that her mother was spiraling into a panic.

When I saw Luz start to worry, I spoke her name very quietly but she didn't hear me.

"Luz," I repeated, somewhat louder, but she continued on her arc of hysteria. When Amparo started getting upset, I went over to Luz and took Amparo from her.

"*¿Luz, que pasó?*"

Finally, she registered my presence and looked at me with a manic intensity.

"*Mami*," she said, "Her eyes are green."

Thirty-Seven

Luz

Shortly after Amparo was born, I started looking at her, studying every inch of her body, worried that some characteristic of the *coyote* would become evident. I was searching for some certainty that, as she grew, she would be safe from his tainted influence.

I often looked at her tiny, delicate hands, tracing the sinewy lines on her palms to see if they matched the lines on mine. I inspected her toes and feet, her forehead and hairline, wondering if these parts of her would grow to match mine. I looked for any evidence that tied her exclusively to me. I often traced the outline of her nose or ears and wondered if they resembled the *coyote's*, or if they would be exclusive replicas of my features.

What of him did she carry inside of her? I worried incessantly that if some part of him manifested in her, that she would be cursed. What if his tainted blood coursed through her veins? Did it matter what kind of mother I was if her father was a monster?

One day, as I was inspecting Amparo, I discovered exactly what I had feared since she was born. Her eyes had changed. They no longer hid behind the deep, dark grey. Somehow, right in front of me, her eyes had transformed to a striking bluish-green. Her dark skin and black hair framed the *coyote's* arresting, terrifying eyes.

How could I look into those eyes, those piercing cat-like eyes, for the rest of my life? My chest tightened with panic as I confronted the *coyote* staring back at me through Amparo's face.

Thirty-Eight

Esperanza

I had noticed that Amparo's eyes had recently started changing. I hadn't said anything to Luz, because I was certain that, in the end, her eyes would be brown, just like everyone in our family. Instead, it was intriguing when they started to go from their original grey, to a greenish-yellow color in the middle, encircled with a dark blue rim around the outside. The change was so gradual that it wasn't obvious unless you were really studying Amparo's eyes. I felt proud that she was developing this unique, distinguishing characteristic.

But when Luz noticed her daughter's new appearance, she became hysterical. At first I didn't understand what had prompted her panic and asked her to explain what was so upsetting. I was holding a crying Amparo as Luz paced back and forth through the apartment, repeating over and over again that her eyes were green.

"Yes, Luz," I said, "she's getting to have really beautiful, mysterious eyes. Isn't that special for Amparo?"

Luz continued frantically racing around our apartment. If she heard what I was saying, she wasn't responding. She continued in this state for several minutes as I worked to calm Amparo down. I prepared a bottle for her, as I sometimes did when Luz was sleeping. Oblivious to what was happening around her, Luz seemed deeply entrenched in something that was unfolding deep within her mind.

As I laid Amparo in the crib, Luz came over to me and grabbed me by the shoulders, pulling me toward her, looking me directly in the eyes.

"*Mami*," she said, "he has those *same* green eyes."

After that, Luz stopped interacting with Amparo. In fact, she stopped interacting with everyone. She stopped eating and spent hour after hour sleeping. It seemed like her brief foray into motherhood was ending as quickly as it had started. She had essentially retreated from the world.

Thirty-Nine

Luz

I finally returned to school in February, when Amparo was about seven months old. I was supposed to return much earlier, but when I started experiencing symptoms of what I would later learn was depression, my mother had called the social worker, looking for help. After spending some time in a hospital, I started going to counseling, along with *mamá*.

Together, with the therapist, we started talking about things that had happened after *mami* left me in the *campo*. Although it was sometimes very painful, it eventually started to feel good to talk through these things *with* my mother.

And eventually, I was able to return to school. The social worker and *mami* had worked together to find childcare for Amparo near our neighborhood so I could easily drop her off and pick her up on my way to and from the bus.

It had been over a year since I had first started school in *los Estados Unidos*. Again, I started well after my classmates began their school year, so I missed the

169

opportunity to make friends with the other new students. By the time I returned, friendships had already been forged. I wasn't hopeful that things would be easy for me.

After so much time away, I dreaded going back there. I felt embarrassed that I had missed so much time. I also felt shame about having had a baby so young. As much as I tried to postpone my return, everyone—the doctors, the social worker, and my mother—knew that it was time to go back. And although I didn't want to admit it, I knew it, too.

As an eighth grader, my first period class was ESOL, a class for students like me, who are speakers of other languages, to learn English. When I walked in, I recognized some of the other students from the year before and wondered if they knew about Amparo. I scanned the classroom, looking for somewhere to sit. The teacher came over to me from behind and put her hands around my shoulders. She tilted her head, smiled warmly at me, and welcomed me into the class. She guided me over to a seat near a front window and asked if I'd like to sit there. Speaking in Spanish, she told me that she was happy to have me in the class and hoped that I felt comfortable there. I nodded at her appreciatively and took the seat she had offered.

I sat my backpack down on the table in front of me and started getting out my notebook and pencil. Two girls seated at a table behind me whispered in Spanish.

"That's Luz," I heard one of them say. "She was new last year, but missed most of the year because she had a baby."

The other girl gasped and I heard her ask her friend how old I was. I imagined the look of shock on her face and was glad that at least I didn't have to see it. They whispered about me for a few more minutes, the first girl relaying some details about me, not getting all the facts right, of course. They quickly tired of my story and moved on to a TV show they had watched the previous evening.

I lowered my head and started writing in my notebook. I didn't know what else to do while waiting for the class to begin, so I started copying from the board. I avoided looking at the other students, but then someone came over and sat down next to me. I pretended not to notice.

"Hi Luz, do you remember me?"

I looked up and over and saw Marisol's friendly smile welcoming me back to school. I tried to hide my embarrassed smile and responded shyly that I did. Although I didn't know Marisol well, I was happy to finally have a class with her. I thought maybe, finally, I would make some friends.

Epilogue

Part 1. Amparo

I'm about to finish first grade! My teacher this year was Mrs. Sanchez. She said that she was very proud of me because I learned to read in two languages. I can speak and read in English *and* Spanish. I feel very proud of myself, too.

Mami is also finishing school, and today we are going to her high school graduation. She looks so beautiful in her white gown and square cap. Yesterday, she tried on her graduation outfit so I could see her in it before everyone else did. She said that the tassel tickled her nose. And she told me that one day I would wear a cap and gown just like hers.

Today, I'm going to the graduation with *Abuela* Esperanza and *abuelita*. *Abuelita* finally came from the *campo* to live with us a few weeks ago. *Mami* and *Tia* Marisol are driving separately. I'm excited to see *mami* receive her diploma, and I'm *really* excited about going out for pizza afterwards!

Part 2. Luz

I'm graduating today! Marisol is on her way over to pick me up to drive me there. When she graduated, two years ago, I drove with her to the ceremony, and we agreed that when it was my turn, she would do the same for me. This promise kept me going, each time I thought I wanted to leave high school.

Marisol has been a blessing over the last few years—she has been my rock since eighth grade. Her friendship has brought me through some very difficult times, and her example has inspired me to keep moving forward. I am so thankful.

Things have not been easy since Amparo was born, and before I got to where I am now, I went through some very challenging times. On more than one occasion, I considered taking my own life. Even now, I continue to see counselors and therapists to work through the traumas that I faced, both on my journey to and after arriving in the United States, and to deal with the depression, anxiety, and the post-traumatic stress disorder I suffered after being raped. I didn't even know that the PTSD was something that happened to people after traumatic events. Learning that the flashbacks and anxiety I was experiencing had a name brought me comfort and allowed me to start moving forward

Over the years, I've taken parenting classes so that I can be the best mother possible to Amparo. My mother and I have participated in workshops for families who have been separated to help us build a stronger, more functional relationship. Slowly, we have come to understand each other more.

Raising a child is not easy. And raising a child conceived the way Amparo was is very, very difficult. Every day is hard.

When Amparo was a baby and I would take her out, I felt the piercing judgment of those around me when they discovered that I was her mother and not her older sister. I would often lower my gaze to avoid seeing the shock on people's faces when I insisted that she was my child. Their embarrassed giggles would echo in my ears, once they were finally convinced.

When strangers would see her beautiful green eyes, they would look at my eyes and then ask if she got them from her father. At first, I didn't know how to respond, but eventually I learned to smile and relay a made-up story involving a distant relative who had that trait. I've finally learned that it's none of anyone's business where her eyes come from, and have stopped responding to their questions.

Getting through school has been very challenging. It took me longer than it should have, but today I am finally graduating from high school and am so proud of this accomplishment. Graduating will be the first thing that I've actually accomplished for myself. It is something that *I* did and not something that was done *to* me.

I know that thousands, maybe even millions, of people graduate from high school every year, and that there are more prestigious accomplishments than that. But for me, my high school diploma represents my strength and fortitude to overcome nearly impossible circumstances. It represents a hope for my future and a certainty that I can decide my role and place in the world.

When I was twelve, my life was turned upside down, my innocence stolen, *mi luz apagada*. It was cruel and unfair. Although, I didn't choose any of it, for many years after, I felt that those events defined me. I felt that I didn't deserve happiness, and even if I did, it was out of my control.

Today, I know better. I know that what happened to me was not my fault. It has taken me a long time, but I am certain now that my light cannot be dimmed.

Secrets of the Moon

ACKNOWLEDGMENTS

To my students, I am eternally grateful for your humble, persuasive examples. Every day, you teach me what it means to prevail. Your fortitude, determination and bravery are an inspiration.

To my mother, Buckie, your constant encouragement carries me through. Your (sometimes ridiculously unfounded) belief in me has made me believe that I am as capable as you told me I was. I love you!

To my father, Bucka, thank you for giving me the gift of laughter. Your sense of humor will be your legacy. Although it is not evident in these pages, it will be mine too. I'm so proud to follow you in a long line of funny people. I love you!

A mi esposo, Nino, me has enseñado paciencia y perseverancia. De ti, he aprendido que cada historia tiene varias versiones y es importante oírlas. Me enseñaste que para poder entender, hay que hacer más que solo escuchar. Gracias por hacer una vida conmigo. Te quiero.

To my children, Nina and Jonas, there are not two people in the world loved as much as you. I am a better person because of you. Thank you for choosing me as your mother and for filling my life with joy and laughter!

To my brother, Joel, your creativity and excitement about anything that interests you inspire me to see the world differently. Thank you for showing me what it means to follow your heart.

To my cousin, Leary, your kindness is a beautiful example to everyone who meets you. Your giving-spirit always sees the best in people and you make me look for the best in them too.

To my friend, Erin Sullivan, I knew you first as a mentor and now as a most trusted friend. Thank you for sharing your wisdom, your energy and your insight with me. Your determination to get things right encourages me to do the same.

To my dear friends, in no particular order, Leah Misbin, Ellen Olsen, Kiran Sandhu, Megan Eiss-Proctor, Shelley Hartford, and Yosselin Marroquin for reading over this manuscript in one or all of its iterations, listening to me talk about it, or generally giving advice. I appreciate how you put up with me!

To my editor, Leah Weiss, your patience and intuition in editing my work have been a gift. You have a magical way of knowing exactly what I mean to say. I am honored and thankful to have worked with you.

ABOUT THE AUTHOR

Tema Encarnación is a teacher of English for Speakers of Other Languages (ESOL) in Annapolis, Maryland.

Tema has worked with other educators in Maryland to start a non-profit organization, the Chesapeake Language Project, which aims to improve post-secondary educational opportunities and access to higher education for immigrant students throughout Maryland.

She lives with her husband and two children outside of Annapolis.

31732044R00111

Made in the USA
Middletown, DE
07 January 2019